LOST WITHOUT LOVE

Elizabeth Raffel

A CANDLELIGHT ECSTASY ROMANCE ®

Published by
Dell Publishing Co., Inc.
1 Dag Hammarskjold Plaza
New York, New York 10017

Copyright © 1983 by Elizabeth Raffel

All rights reserved. No part of this book may be
reproduced or transmitted in any form or by any
means, electronic or mechanical, including photocopying,
recording, or by any information storage
and retrieval system, without the written permission
of the Publisher, except where permitted by law.

Dell ® TM 681510, Dell Publishing Co., Inc.

Candlelight Ecstasy Romance®, 1,203,540, is a registered
trademark of Dell Publishing Co., Inc.,
New York, New York.

ISBN: 0-440-15100-7

Printed in the United States of America
First printing—October 1983

To Our Readers:

We have been delighted with your enthusiastic response to Candlelight Ecstasy Romances®, and we thank you for the interest you have shown in this exciting series.

In the upcoming months we will continue to present the distinctive sensuous love stories you have come to expect only from Ecstasy. We look forward to bringing you many more books from your favorite authors and also the very finest work from new authors of contemporary romantic fiction.

As always, we are striving to present the unique, absorbing love stories that you enjoy most—books that are more than ordinary romance.

Your suggestions and comments are always welcome. Please write to us at the address below.

Sincerely,

The Editors
Candlelight Romances
1 Dag Hammarskjold Plaza
New York, New York 10017

CHAPTER ONE

Lauren McCloud rolled the window further down and undid several buttons at the neck of her shirt. The cool breeze whipping into her red Subaru was a welcome relief from the sun, beating down on Interstate 75 as it entered the state of Georgia. Though she was tired after her long trip, fatigue couldn't repress the exhilaration she felt at seeing the crisp green of spring all around.

She was amazed by the transformation in scenery. Less than thirty-six hours ago she had left Connecticut wrapped in snow and ice. The rural landscape had resembled a huge, magnificent still-life, frozen in a palette of white, grays, and muted blues. In the past she had always loved this magnificent sight, sometimes sketching it from her bedroom window. But this year it only oppressed her. She had gotten tired of winter. And the latest storm had filled her with desperation as nature's unending bleakness seemed to reinforce the sadness consuming her heart.

The driving had been so treacherous, her father had begged her to postpone the trip for at least a couple of days. The arrangements had only been made three weeks ago, anyway. Surely the papers her sister Susan had to sign could wait. But it was no use. He knew that was not the main reason for her trip. Under normal circumstances Lauren would have been happy to ease her father's mind. In fact she was pleased with herself for waiting as long as she had. If it hadn't been for her dissertation defense, she would have left a month ago—right after she and David had stopped seeing each other. But the doctorate had been a long haul—indeed, the entire length of her relationship with David. To let it drag on would have been self-defeating. Two days ago she had done her defense. Once it was over, the thought of staying was more than she could bear. Everything around her only reminded her of David and, of course, there was always the problem of running into him. She couldn't face it. Or him. Not now.

Her father had gone out on his tractor, in the freezing rain, to plough the long driveway that curved out to the road. He had done it without complaint. Even as she drove along the Georgia highway, she could see the mixture of hope and fear in his eyes—hope that this trip would help to heal the wounds of love his younger daughter was suffering from, and fear for Lauren's safety. Her mother had died in a horrible automobile accident when Lauren was four and Susan was nine, during a storm much like this one. It was a tragedy that had haunted him ever since, though he seldom spoke of it.

The job of being both father and mother to two young girls might have intimidated a lesser man. But John McCloud was a very special person. He had raised the girls on his own, never giving a second's notice to all the advice relatives offered. Send the girls to live with Aunt Sally, she'll know how to raise them. Send them to boarding school, the discipline will do them good. On and on it came, for the first couple of years after their mother's death, all of it different but the message the same— break up the family. John McCloud carried on as if he'd done the job all his life. And Lauren had loved him more than she could say for doing just that, for trying to preserve the family life she had known. That was why she had always loved the farm. It reminded her of all his effort and of all his caring. She remembered how he had even learned to pick out attractive girls' clothing for birthdays and Christmas. This quiet man, who had been a farmer all his life, turned out to have very sensitive taste when it came to his daughters. Susan got brightly colored outfits. Lauren wore pastels and subtler shades. The girls had always been that different.

Before she reached adolescence, Lauren hadn't noticed the differences much. Of course, she had looked up to Susan, frequently wishing she could be just like her older sister; she had assumed she would indeed be like Susan when she grew up.

But by the time she was eleven, it all began to change. She suddenly began to really notice all Susan's friends—especially her boyfriends. There were a lot of them, and they were always the handsomest boys in the huge high school, five miles from the McCloud farm. And they all drove flashy cars. Not a morning passed when Susan wasn't picked up and driven to school. Weekends were a foregone conclusion—Susan always had dates both Friday and Saturday nights. With boys and girls alike her manner was the same: always relaxed and entertaining. She never ran out of cute or funny things to say, and if she did say something catty or nasty it was just at the right moment. Everyone would laugh and agree. Nothing embarrassed her. Nothing intimidated her. She was the very center of an elite group, and everyone worshipped her.

It was about this time that Lauren began to notice the fights between Susan and her father. Susan never obeyed curfews. If Mr. McCloud had the effrontery to catch her coming in late, she refused to apologize, claiming he was unreasonable and overprotective. If these confrontations turned into yelling matches, which they frequently did, Lauren could overhear her father saying things about Susan's reputation.

Lauren had tried very hard to ignore this conflict—she hated being torn between the two people she cared about most in the world. But as time passed, she began to have her own personal problems with Susan. Lauren began to look like Susan. There were differences: Susan's hair was a true blond, while Lauren's was honey colored. Susan's hair was straight, while Lauren's fell in loose, graceful waves. But their faces were almost identical: smooth, fair-complexioned ovals, dominated by large almond-shaped eyes and naturally deep rose-colored lips that always made them look as though they were wearing lipstick. The only physical difference was eye color. Susan's were deep velvety brown, warm and passionate in their intensity, and Lauren's were a bright vivid aquamarine blue, cool and intelligent.

The problem arose at school. Susan had left high school only the year before Lauren began. Her memory was still very much alive there, and everyone expected Lauren to pick up where Susan had left off. Initially, Lauren was flattered by the comparison, but the expectations soon began to weigh on her. Her nature was quieter and more sensitive. She preferred painting to partying, and she didn't particularly like crowds. When, after a few months, it became clear that she not only wouldn't but couldn't pick up Susan's torch, she began to resent living in Susan's shadow. She didn't want to be a "failed Susan." She wanted to be herself. She decided to be as different from Susan as she could, concentrating all her energies on school. She seldom dated, partly because she was so shy and partly because her straight A's intimidated many of the boys she found attractive. By the time she graduated from high school, she had long since come to consider herself cold and intellectual, the exact opposite of her sister.

Lauren's college years did little to change this image. She did follow in Susan's footsteps, going to the same large state college. But Susan had graduated and taken a job with an advertising agency in New York, and the college itself was so big that she had not left an indelible impression. For the first time in her life Lauren felt really free to be herself.

Her classes were fascinating; her fellow students were even more so. In no time at all she had formed a group of friends who shared her interests. And she began to date the young men who joked around with her, walking to and from classes. Lauren loved the attention. She took pleasure in the endless stream of compliments, almost surprised to discover how many people thought she was beautiful. She enjoyed the warm friendship, going to plays, concerts, and football games with people who shared her feelings. And yet she always held back. Part of her couldn't return amorous overtures. A good-night kiss, an arm around her shoulders—that was as far as she felt able to go.

For a while she worried about it. After all, many of her friends were having very intimate relationships with their boyfriends. But she always resolved her doubts by assuring herself that she hadn't had much experience with boys in high school, and she simply had to follow the course of her own feelings. And then, of course, there were her career ambitions. Psychology was her favorite subject. There were many job opportunities available, but all of them required a graduate degree. If she was going to enter graduate school, which would require long hours of intense study, she would have to be very careful not to get encumbered by a deep relationship. How many of the young men she was dating now would themselves go on to graduate school? And, if not, how many of them would be understanding of a girl friend with such ambitions?

She thought long and hard on this whole subject and was finally quite pleased with her seemingly innate ability not to get too involved. She seldom spoke of this, even to her closest girl friends, but some of them seemed to guess what her feelings were and admired her self-control. They often remarked on how lucky she was not to get hurt, as many of them had been. These sentiments only made Lauren feel more sure of herself, a sureness that had grown slowly but steadily since she had entered college. When graduation arrived, she was filled with a sense of triumph. Not only had she graduated *cum laude*, but she had received her acceptance to an extremely prestigious graduate program at a private college not far from her father's farm. It seemed as if every dream she had ever had was coming true. Her future seemed full and settled—graduate school, and then a career. Men were actually the last thing on her list of priorities, not forgotten entirely by any means, but more or less on hold until everything else was taken care of.

Then, something happened that summer to change her feelings. Even now, almost five years later, with all the experiences of a grown woman, the memory of this incident brought a rush of color to Lauren's cheeks. In a self-conscious gesture her hand moved nervously from the steering wheel to brush the hair from her forehead. And, as always, the embarrassment turned to anger.

"Damn that Chad Bently," she muttered, though only she could hear it.

But it had been as much her fault as his, and she knew it. A sinking feeling filled her head and stomach as memories of that day—Susan's wedding day—rushed into her tired mind.

The news of Susan's engagement had caught Lauren completely by surprise. After the flurry of final exams, and the excitement of graduation, she had been looking forward to a quiet summer. Suddenly she had to deal with all the excitement of preparing for a July wedding. Susan wanted to have the ceremony in the rose garden, behind the farmhouse; in order to have everything just perfect, she was leaving work two weeks before the ceremony, to come home and take care of the preparations herself.

Susan's return home was marked by constant parties and festivities. All her old friends rallied round, for what promised to be *the* wedding of the season. Though Lauren was to be maid of honor, she felt very much out of place. It was almost as if she were back in high school again, surrounded by people who expected her to be just like Susan, only younger, smaller, less important. All her own excitement about graduating, and going on to graduate school, suddenly seemed inconsequential.

She had never gotten over feeling a strange mixture of admiration and jealousy for Susan, though she had done her best to hide it on the very rare occasions when her sister did come home from New York for a weekend.

When Greg Bently, her sister's fiancé, did arrive, Lauren realized what all the fuss was about. To begin with he was tall, dark, and handsome. On top of that he had a brilliant future as a geologist, would travel all over the world, and it was obvious that he absolutely adored the ground that Susan walked on. Once again Susan had succeeded brilliantly. And, once again, Lauren found herself wondering about her own ambitions. With a week to go before the wedding, she found herself longing with all her heart for the whole thing to be over with. Longing to have the farm back to herself, as a quiet place of relaxation and reflection. The only thing that made her feel differently was seeing how pleased her father was to have Susan around. He'd missed her so, even though he'd tried to let her lead her own life.

Not that having Susan back was easy. On the one hand she

wanted the wedding to be perfect. On the other she seemed to find every detail a constant imposition. Lauren couldn't figure her sister out—not at all. Marriage was supposed to be a happy event, full of satisfaction with the present and hope for the future. And, as Lauren got to know Greg, she realized how lucky Susan really was. Lauren couldn't help but wish that she had someone as thoughtful and considerate—and as understanding—as Greg madly in love with her. But Susan seemed to take all that for granted.

As the days dragged on and the wedding day approached, Lauren was aware of a subtle sense of anticipation growing in Susan. At first she assumed, naturally enough, that Susan was excited about the wedding. But then something happened to change her thinking. As she sat on the porch one evening, she overheard Susan and Greg talking. As usual Susan was giving him a hard time about everything under the sun. Then, in what initially passed for a teasing tone, she said, "Maybe I should really be marrying Chad. He'd never have any problem getting himself organized."

The remark bothered Lauren; it seemed yet another example of her sister's selfishness. And yet Lauren found herself wondering about Chad Bently. He was Greg's older brother, who lived in California, where he ran a construction company. That was literally all she knew about him, other than the fact that he was to be best man at the wedding and, therefore, probably her partner for dancing. He was to arrive the next day, only two days before the wedding. All the rest of that evening, before his arrival, she had trouble getting her mind off him. Susan hadn't really said anything about him—nothing at all. Yet, just the fact that she had made that comment upset Lauren. And it gave her a very disturbing feeling about Chad Bently.

The next day found Susan more cantankerous than ever. She took longer than usual to dress, then complained bitterly when she discovered she had missed her appointment for the final fitting on her wedding dress. When it turned out that the only other time open for the fitting was two o'clock, all hell broke loose. Susan ranted and raved at the dressmaker for a solid ten minutes. All to no avail. If she wouldn't come in at two, there was no way the dressmaker could promise to see her before the wedding. Furious but resigned, Susan finally agreed. It wasn't until she and Greg were going out the door, at one o'clock, that Susan spoke to Lauren. She hurried her younger sister off to the side of the room, away from Greg.

"Be sure you're here until I get back," she whispered anxiously. "Chad is arriving early. He'll be here around two, and I don't want him left alone with Dad. He'll be bored to death. At least you know how to carry on a conversation."

Lauren nodded a little dubiously, but Susan didn't seem to notice. A minute later Susan and Greg were gone. With growing misgivings Lauren watched them speed away in Greg's red Porsche. Then her mind went back to the nasty remark Susan had made about their father. John McCloud might not be a city slicker, but he was an intelligent, sensitive human being who had the sense not to talk unless he had something to say. If Chad Bently didn't care for that kind of person, then he wouldn't like her either, she thought. And, for that matter, she wouldn't like him.

The more she thought about it, the angrier she got. The angrier she got, the more determined she was not to stay in the house to save Chad Bently the supreme embarrassment of having to talk to her father. She had been planning on going for a walk, anyway. Why should she change her plans, just for Susan? This was the first afternoon in two weeks that Susan hadn't tied her up, doing any number of tiresome little chores, for which Lauren never received so much as a thank-you.

She ran upstairs to change out of the skirt she was wearing. It wasn't rugged enough for a stroll through the fields. She pulled on a pair of old cutoffs she'd owned for years and was surprised to discover they were somewhat tighter than they used to be. She laughed, realizing that she'd worn them before her figure had fully matured. Actually, though they were a little indecent, it was amazing she could still fit into them at all. Then she pulled on a white polo shirt, tucked it into the cutoffs, and completed the outfit with a favorite hemp belt. Glancing in the mirror, she smiled to see how young she looked.

She ran back downstairs and was halfway out the door before she realized she hadn't told her father about her plans. But he was nowhere in sight, so she simply scribbled a note and dropped it on the kitchen table.

Minutes later she was out in the fields behind the farmhouse. Fields that seemed to stretch for miles in every direction. Fields that she'd known like the back of her hand, since the time she could first walk. Though she knew she would probably have to work in a city, she always imagined having a home in an area much like this one. Here, there was peace and tranquility. And there was time. Time to think; time to enjoy small things.

She could never understand how she had ended up loving the country so much, while Susan had ended up hating it. She shrugged. What did it matter? It was a good thing women were mobile enough these days to go where they wanted to go. Susan would probably always live in a city, and she would be happy there. Lauren would always return to the country, no matter how many cities she visited.

She wandered this way and that, always sure that she knew her way back but not paying much attention to the exact direction. Finally, she noticed fence posts ahead. She stood still for a moment, then realized she'd actually walked all the way to the old post road. It wasn't the most direct route to her father's house, and it was seldom ever traveled. But years ago she had spent many a hot summer day exploring this neighborhood. She quickened her pace. When she reached the fence, she placed her hand on the only spot she knew to be splinter free and vaulted over onto the dusty surface. It wasn't until she was standing in the middle of the road that she noticed a man in a reclining position on the grass opposite her. Her eyes widened.

"Who are you?" she exclaimed, more surprised than upset by the sudden intrusion.

For a moment he didn't speak or move. He continued twiddling the long piece of field grass between his fingers, scrutinizing her with an amused expression. Lauren placed her hands on her hips, to register her growing impatience.

"Are you mute?" she finally suggested in a mildly exasperated tone. "Don't speak, please. Just nod and I'll understand."

A smile flickered across his face. He pushed himself forward into a full sitting position.

"Just momentarily struck dumb," he replied in a deep voice not untouched by a wry humor. "That was quite a little performance you just put on."

"You've never seen anyone jump a fence before?" She laughed.

"Not anyone like you," he said quietly, allowing his eyes to review the shapely line revealed by her tight shorts. And not just once. They moved slowly over her, again and again, making a very blatant assessment of her slim figure. "I'm not used to seeing quite so much . . . natural beauty." His gaze left her only momentarily, to encompass the wide open fields and blue sky.

She nodded, crossing her arms over her chest. "And all this natural beauty has overwhelmed you so completely that you can't think?"

He shrugged. "What do I have to think about?"

"I asked you a question," she pressed him.

He laughed and shrugged again. "I can't remember what it was" was the annoyingly nonchalant reply.

Lauren shook her head, feeling even more exasperated. But when her eyes met his again, it was clear her impatience was having no effect. Indeed, it only seemed to add to his amusement. And, as she stared at him, she had to admit he was very attractive. And, yes, oddly familiar. She couldn't figure out why. She knew she had never met him but . . . the dark tanned features, even the proportions of his body, the broad muscular chest covered by the white business shirt, his arms uncovered by rolled-up sleeves, dark and muscular—for some reason he looked familiar.

It wasn't that he was handsome, in the strict sense. It was simply that, taken as a whole, he had a strangely powerful attractiveness. If it had been someone she knew she might have been embarrassed by the blatant provocativeness of his stare. But then again, nobody she knew would have stared at her this way. It was a new experience to be looked at as a mature woman. And she was enjoying the attention. But enough was enough. It was getting a little ridiculous. After all, he *was* an absolute stranger. She forced a more serious expression to her face.

"Well, what are you doing here?"

"Just enjoying the view," he said, still smiling. He stood up slowly, as though he didn't have a care in the world, picked up the suit jacket, flung it over his shoulder, and walked toward her, a lazy, relaxed stride.

"You can enjoy it from a distance," she said, trying to hide the slight alarm caused by his advance.

He laughed, stopping not five feet away. "Don't look so scared —I gave up attacking teen-agers for my New Year's resolution."

For a second Lauren thought of protesting the comment about her age, but decided against it. What did it matter what he thought? To say nothing of the fact that she no longer wanted to prolong the conversation. She was getting fidgety having him even this close. She took a couple of steps back.

"I'm leaving now," she stammered. "I don't have all afternoon to chat."

He looked around again, as casually as if he were checking the sky for rain.

"Actually," he remarked, his eyes, with their full dark gray intensity, coming back to her face, "now that I've had such an enchanting rest, I think I'll go, too." He paused, making an obvious attempt to suppress a smile. "There's just one problem."

"What's that?" she responded with relief.

"You've been such a charming companion I hate to impose on you still further, but you see, I'm lost."

Lauren shook her head. "I don't believe that for one second," she exclaimed.

He shrugged again. "Believe what you like. I came from California this morning, and I've been trying to find the McCloud farm." He reached into his pants pocket and handed her a small piece of paper. "I was given these instructions, but I ended up here. I've been up and down this road three times. I can't find the place."

She quickly unfolded the paper and began to study it, more to hide her surprise than anything else. Yes, it was all beginning to make sense. And it was rather comical, too. The map was impossible. Clearly Susan had drawn it. No one could have failed to get lost, following such inept instructions. So this was . . . She looked up at him, trying to keep a straight face.

"You're lucky I happened to come this way," she said, her voice slightly less rigid and forbidding.

"Are you going to say this road is never traveled?" he said, smiling back.

"It really isn't. I haven't been this way in years, myself."

He nodded as if to say he didn't believe a word she was saying. Lauren ignored him.

"Let's see," she said, pointing back toward the car. "Go back to the county line and take it to your right, about a mile and a half. Turn right again, then take the first right onto the dirt road. Follow it all the way in, until you see the red brick farmhouse."

"Thank you ever so much," he said, making a motion as though he were tipping a hat to her. "I appreciate your warm hospitality."

With those words he strode down the road, back to his car. When he pulled away in a cloud of dust, Lauren began to giggle. She continued on her walk in good spirits, returning to the house a couple of hours later. By then Susan was back and the sounds of merriment and celebration were strong. Lauren sneaked up the back stairs, changed into a sundress, and stayed in her room till dinner. Susan finally came to get her. She was more excited than Lauren had seen her in years . . . but she was a little angry, too.

"Where did you go?" she demanded.

Lauren didn't look her sister in the eye. She just shrugged.

"Oh, nowhere. Something came up and I had to go out."

"Well," Susan replied with exaggerated exasperation, "it's okay. I can tell Chad didn't mind talking to Dad."

"I'm so relieved," Lauren answered with feigned concern. "It would have been horrible if he had."

The two women walked downstairs. Lauren could see the dining room table, all beautifully set. She could see Greg, her father, and the stranger from the post road sitting around it, talking and laughing. She swallowed hard just before entering. She wanted to keep a straight face. Susan swooped into the room ahead of her, like the grand dame of the house. She never so much as looked at Greg. She had eyes only for Chad.

"Chad," she exclaimed. The second she spoke, he looked up and as he did his eyes lighted on Lauren standing in the doorway. At first there was surprise in his eyes; then a dazzling smile passed over his face. Susan glanced back at Lauren in confusion, then continued as if nothing had happened. "This is my younger sister, Lauren—the brains of the family. Remember, I told you about her?"

Chad kept looking at Lauren. They advanced toward each other and shook hands—a firm businesslike shake that lasted just a little longer than necessary.

"How could I forget your description of her?" he said, glancing back at Susan. "It was so accurate I have the feeling I've already met her." His gaze shifted to Lauren's face. She could see the humor in his eyes. She swept past him.

"It's nice to meet you, Chad. No one ever described you to me, but it's funny. It almost seems as though we have met before—somewhere."

"It sounds as though you two will make a lovely couple at the wedding," Susan observed, sitting down. But Lauren could hear the discomfort in her sister's voice.

The meal passed, perfectly amicable on the surface. But beneath it all, several antagonistic currents were flowing. Susan kept trying to converse only with Chad, while he, for his part, seemed to be always trying to shift the conversation to include everyone. And every now and then his eyes would meet Lauren's. She would smile, all sweetness and light, answering all his questions about her schooling and ambitions, politely—oh, so politely.

Immediately following dinner Lauren excused herself on the grounds of fatigue. It was an odd game she was playing with Chad; but that in itself wouldn't have made her leave. What she couldn't deal with was Susan's behavior. How could Greg possibly tolerate it? And what had Chad done to earn such devotion? It made her determinedly suspicious of him.

The rehearsal day seemed endless. Luckily, the hothouse atmosphere of the previous evening was broken by the presence of all the bridesmaids, and by the arrival of Greg and Chad's parents. But though Lauren herself made a large effort to keep some distance between herself and Chad, she couldn't help noticing the effect he was having on all the other girls. They flocked around him, flirting outrageously. And the star flirter was none other than the bride herself. Lauren seethed as she watched. She made herself wander over to talk to Greg. The least she could do was distract him, so he wouldn't have to watch.

To her surprise, not to say amazement, Greg seemed totally unconcerned. In fact she could tell by the smile on his face that he found Susan's behavior genuinely amusing. So, in the end, to keep from having to watch the spectacle, she kept to herself, taking every excuse offered to avoid the crowd. It wasn't till the actual rehearsal that her presence was absolutely necessary. And by seven o'clock that evening, as the rehearsal started, she was relieved that she hadn't had to say more than "Good morning" to Chad. As soon as rehearsal was over, she would slip up to her room, avoiding the wedding party altogether. She was sure her absence wouldn't be noticed.

But the rehearsal was not short. Everyone humored Susan's mania for perfection, and no one complained, but there were tired smiles among the crowd when it was finally over, at nine thirty. Again, Lauren had been lucky. Through all of the practicing Chad had been too busy chatting with the other bridesmaids to notice her. She was just slipping into the house when Susan called after her.

"Lauren? Come back here."

She almost didn't, but then she realized it would be unforgivably rude. She glanced over her shoulder, to see Susan standing with two bridesmaids, Becky Walton and Trisha Jordan. She sighed with relief. At least Chad was nowhere in sight. She walked reluctantly back. Susan grabbed her arm and pulled her into the small group.

"Lauren," she scolded, "I didn't ask you to be my maid of honor for no reason. I can't possibly entertain Chad every minute. You're going to have to take care of him tonight *and* tomorrow and keep him away from all these lascivious women. I know he'll be safe with you."

Lauren was just on the verge of telling her sister to go jump in the lake, when another more satisfying thought occurred to her. She would show Susan just how *safe* an escort she could be. She smiled perfunctorily at the others, disengaging her arm from Susan's.

"Well," she pronounced, "I guess I'd better go about my assigned course of business."

Music was playing, people were beginning to dance. Lauren didn't stop to notice. Her eyes were searching everywhere for Chad. She wandered from group to group, asking as she went. This was not something she was prepared to give up on. There was a principle at stake. Finally she found him, just walking away from a small group that included his parents. He stood absolutely still as soon as he saw her. He was dressed in a pair of casual tan pants and a white polo shirt open at the neck. A wicked smile flashed across his face.

"Well," he said slowly, "you're the last person I was expecting to see again. I was surprised you even came to rehearsal. Little Miss Hospitality herself."

Lauren just smiled back. "I hope to make it all up to you tonight. Shall we dance?"

Chad shrugged as though it didn't matter one way or another, and for a second Lauren's insides tightened. Maybe she didn't know enough about men to pull this thing off. She threw her shoulder back slightly, holding out her hand. She sensed just a bit of reluctance in his grip. Did he find her that unattractive? The way he had looked at her the day before hadn't made her think so, but now she was growing increasingly less sure.

When they joined the crowd of dancers, the music was very slow. Lauren wasn't about to let this opportunity pass. She swung gracefully toward him, only to be pleasantly surprised when his arm slipped easily around her waist. They danced slowly, their bodies moving together to the rhythm. But he didn't pull her close. Susan and Greg drifted past. Susan smiled.

"See what a nice time you're having, Lauren? Chad's such a gentleman." And her eyes lighted possessively on her fiancé's brother.

Lauren slipped one of her arms from Chad's shoulder to his waist, allowing her fingers to stray down his chest. She glanced seductively into his eyes, smiling with feigned shyness.

"We seem so far apart," she whispered coyly.

Chad scrutinized her. Alternate looks of amusement and confusion passed through his eyes. Lauren didn't wait for an answer. She reached up with both arms, winding them around his neck.

"I wasn't under the impression that you had any trouble knowing how to treat a girl. . . ." Her voice trailed off as he suddenly looked down at her. His lips seemed to be hovering just above hers. His eyes glistened—dark, mysterious, full of unspoken promises. The music, the night, the stars, the faint smell of whatever scent it was he had splashed on his face, and the feel of his firm body, now pressing against hers, all of it combined to make her feel dizzy and, yes, very happy. She moved even closer, still staring up into his deep eyes. They no longer looked so questioning. She had made herself perfectly clear. She and Chad seemed to be drifting together on some timeless plane. It was at least a minute or more, after the music stopped, before he stepped away from her. But one of his hands remained on her shoulder; his eyes never left her face. Then they were walking toward the bar.

Chad ordered a Scotch and turned to Lauren.

"Are you old enough to drink?" he said with just a hint of amazement in his voice.

She smiled confidently. "How old do you think I am?"

Chad ran his fingers through his hair and looked away. When he looked back, he seemed quite unnerved.

"Going by what I saw yesterday, I'd say sixteen."

She reached out, placing her hand on his bare arm. She squeezed the firm flesh.

"Wouldn't you be in trouble if I were?" she whispered in suggestive tones.

He shook his head and smiled.

"How old *are* you?"

"Twenty-two."

His sigh was almost audible. He studied her face; a sly smile crept across his. His message was clear. That covered the whole situation. He was dealing with an experienced woman.

"What would you like?" he asked.

"White wine."

Drinks in hand, they wandered away from the crowd, around the side of the huge old house, to a screened-in porch. Lauren sat down on the steps. Chad joined her.

For a long time they said nothing. They sipped the cool drinks and reveled in the beauty of their surroundings. The wine seemed to pour fire into Lauren's veins. She felt more attractive than ever before—and more in command of the situation. After all, this had all been part of her plan. It was coming off beautifully. She reached out and placed her hand on Chad's knee. She smiled to herself and then giggled; Chad looked at her with genuine amazement in his eyes.

"You are some young lady," he whispered in a husky tone, full of an exciting urgency.

Lauren tossed her head back, staring him in the face.

"You're making a big mistake," she cooed playfully.

There was a small silence. She continued to toy with his leg.

"Oh, yeah? What?" he said slowly.

Lauren leaned very close to him. Her breasts brushed against his arm.

"I'm not a lady. I'm a woman. There's a big difference."

Chad nodded, then in a slow, sure movement, drew her to him. His touch was so powerful, his body so warm, Lauren's head swam slightly. His lips hovered above hers, tantalizing her senses, filling her with a yearning she had never felt before, a sense of triumph. She, as a woman, had succeeded in arousing him. And when his mouth lowered to hers, slowly, everything seemed so slow, and his lips pressed against hers, at first gently, but then with growing urgency, and she couldn't resist the need to return his kiss. Her lips parted willingly, welcoming his tongue into the warm moistness of her mouth. She had never been kissed so completely, so passionately. She had never felt any of the feelings now consuming every other thought.

It wasn't until they started to lean back, lying down on the porch, it wasn't until his hand felt the warm curve of her breast, and moved toward the buttons of her blouse, that she came out of the reeling sensation long enough to realize what was happening. Thrill and triumph were suddenly replaced by fear. She was letting an absolute stranger, a man she'd known barely a day, touch her the way she had never permitted anyone else. The fact that his hands aroused such yearning passion, making her whole body ache for more, meant nothing. What was she doing? Had she lost her senses? How could she have imagined she could go through with it? She started to pull frantically away.

"No, no," she cried. "Not here. Not now."

Chad tried to pull her back, but then let her move away. He looked confused, but gradually his features composed.

"You're right," he said quietly, his voice still husky with passion. "There *are* too many people around."

Lauren curled her legs under her, brushed her hair back, and started to stand up.

"I can't," she said hoarsely, fighting back frightened tears.

There was a brief silence, during which a thousand looks seemed to pass through Chad's eyes, but mostly there was confusion.

"You can't?" he pressed her.

She shook her head, not daring to speak.

"But you were the one who started this whole thing," he snapped angrily. "You can't lead a man on like this and then say 'I can't.'"

Lauren stared helplessly at him.

Just at that moment Trisha and her date came quietly around the corner. Trisha burst into giggles as soon as she saw Chad.

"I hope we're not interrupting anything." She flashed a knowing smile at both Chad and Lauren.

"As a matter of fact," Chad began, but he never got to finish. Lauren smoothed her skirt and walked toward the side door.

"As a matter of fact," she replied coolly, avoiding Chad's presence, "I was just going inside. I'm very tired."

But sleep did not come easily to her that night, and when it did come, it was fitful. By morning she was more agitated than she'd been the night before. She would have to see Chad today; try as she might, she couldn't imagine what she should or could do or say. As far as she was concerned, the only thing she had to be grateful for was that Trisha had not come around the corner of the house five minutes earlier.

The wedding wasn't until two, so she lay in bed until eleven, wrestling with her problem and with her conscience. By rights she knew she owed Chad an apology. She should walk firmly downstairs and make a clean breast of it, admit she was in the wrong and, if he was the least bit sympathetic, tell him why she had done it. Yes, that was what she would do. She couldn't think about it another minute, or she'd go crazy. She hopped out of bed, threw on a pair of shorts and a T-shirt, and was about to leave the room when Susan entered without knocking, an angry scowl on her face.

"Good morning, Sue," Lauren said lightly, trying to ease the tension in the air.

"Look, Lauren, Trish told me about what happened between you and Chad last night," Susan said abruptly.

"I don't know what you're talking about."

"Look, Lauren, at least have the honesty to admit it."

"There's nothing to admit. Nothing. If you don't believe me, ask Chad." Lauren pulled off her T-shirt and shorts and grabbed her robe. She walked out of the room toward the bathroom. Susan followed.

"Well, I don't care what actually happened," Susan snapped.

"It's your own business. But don't ruin my wedding carrying on like that in a crowd."

Lauren spun around as the words exploded from her mouth. "How dare you criticize my behavior! You don't care what happened between Chad and me? Who are you kidding? Especially after the way you were throwing yourself at Chad while everyone was looking on!"

Susan tossed her head back, glaring angrily at her sister. "Well, at least we know where we stand with each other. I've never made any bones about what I was up to. But you . . . with all your pretense of being holier than thou! I should have guessed years ago. I'm just sorry I asked you to be my maid of honor. I should have given the pleasure to a real friend—someone I could trust."

With that she stormed out of the bathroom.

Lauren took a long, long bath to try to cool herself down. She had never imagined anything like this happening between herself and Susan, but in many ways it was inevitable. And at least it *was* out in the open. At least they did know where they stood with each other. The only other result of this explosion was that she now had two difficult relationships to handle today, instead of one.

And then, of course, she wasn't sure if she'd have the chance to apologize to Chad before the wedding. She sighed wearily. And, when she slipped into her bridesmaid's dress, she felt no better. She had completely forgotten that the pink frothy creation had a low neckline that revealed her full bust. This was the last thing she needed. Trisha and Becky would love the opportunity to show off their bodies. But after last night Lauren just wanted to shrink into a corner and hide.

Finally, she took hold of herself. She wasn't a little girl anymore. She was a woman. And she would handle the situation. She would keep her distance. That was all there was to it. All she had to do was get through the afternoon. Surely the reception would be over by six, because Susan and Greg were catching a seven o'clock plane. And once Chad was gone, she'd never have to see him for the rest of her life. She could push the whole horrid memory as far back in her mind as possible. Ultimately, she would simply forget it.

When she returned to the living room at one thirty, Becky and Trisha were waiting. They went out of their way to be nice to her. Not another word was said about the evening before, and Chad was nowhere in sight. The crowd outside was growing by the minute. Finally, through the window, Lauren saw Greg and Chad standing to one side of the rose garden, chatting and laughing. She felt a wave of relief. Chad was obviously not still sulking. He couldn't have been all that upset. She'd just pretend nothing had happened. That was one problem out of the way.

Susan descended only minutes before the ceremony was to start. She was a stunning bride. The dress, the veil, her hair, her makeup—everything was perfect. Yet, deep in her eyes, Lauren could still see the anger flashing. Trisha and Becky rushed over to ooh and ahh. Susan never so much as glanced at Lauren. She simply pretended her younger sister didn't exist. Just as well, Lauren thought. It simplified everything. If Susan avoided her, there would be no further possibility of conflict. That second her father came in, dressed in his tuxedo. He smiled cheerily, they formed the line they'd practiced at rehearsal, with John and Susan McCloud at the back, preceded by the three bridesmaids, and walked out in the hot summer sun to the romantic strains of "We've Only Just Begun."

The ceremony seemed to whiz by. Chad's eyes met Lauren's when she first appeared, and for a second she thought they were lingering a little too long on her neckline. But then she pushed the thought out of her mind. Surely, after last night, he would avoid her like the plague. Once or twice, during the ceremony, she thought she felt him staring at her. But modesty dictated that she keep looking straight ahead, or at least down at her feet.

She was staring straight ahead, when the bride and groom were answering their vows. Greg responded quickly. Susan was not quite so prompt. And, during that moment of hesitation, Lauren saw without a doubt that her sister's eyes flickered over to Chad's face. He smiled very slightly—a knowing smile, Lauren thought. Then, Susan finally said "I do," and the wedding was over—to the sounds of music, laughter, and a few tears. Lauren sighed with relief. One stage was over. And all in all, it had come off pretty well.

CHAPTER TWO

Lauren took her place at the head table. She had hurried over ahead of everyone else, feeling the need for a quiet moment to herself. It wasn't that she was nervous about having to sit beside Chad. Probably nothing more than fatigue was making her feel so edgy. She hadn't had much sleep the night before, after all. And then, of course, the argument with Susan had left her feeling very keyed up. She took a couple of deep breaths and stared up at the blue, blue sky. It was a perfect day for a wedding. Everything would be fine. In fact she would take the opportunity to apologize to Chad.

People began to drift in, drinks in hand. Many of them smiled at Lauren, commenting on how beautiful she looked. But it seemed that at least half an hour passed before the rest of the bridal party arrived. And when they walked in, Chad had Becky on one arm and Trisha on the other. They advanced toward the platform, all smiles and laughter. Chad's eyes met Lauren's. And, oddly enough, Lauren felt his smile was really directed at her. He thought her amusing. He looked at her for several long minutes, but never so much as said hi.

Staring back into his deep, dark eyes, Lauren had a sick feeling in the pit of her stomach. Had she made that much of a fool of herself? She was just fighting to control the panic welling up inside, when Susan's voice interrupted her.

"Lauren," Susan said sweetly, too sweetly in fact, "I've changed the seating arrangements—you'll be sitting at the end of the table—down where Becky was supposed to sit." Susan laughed, pointing over at Chad, Becky, and Trisha. "It's just that

Chad's having such a good time with Trisha and Becky. I hate to break them up."

Lauren snatched her bouquet from the table and walked quietly, but determinedly, away from the gathering crowd. She couldn't feel the warm sun or the entrancing breeze wafting the scent of a thousand roses through the air. All she could feel was anger. She entered the house and started up the stairs. She was almost at the top when it occurred to her how ridiculously she was behaving. She couldn't let Susan push her around like this. By running into the house she was playing right into Susan's hands—and further reinforcing her image with everyone, most especially Chad, as an immature little girl.

She raced into the bathroom, combed her hair, and freshened her face with cool water. Then she stared at herself in the mirror, with a new sense of confidence. She would go back, she would enjoy herself, and she would take the first possible opportunity offered to make her apology to Chad. She had been foolish the night before—foolish and arrogant. He had every reason to smile at her as though she were an amusing child. That was the way she had acted. She couldn't hope to right the situation completely, but at least she could give the impression that she wasn't totally ignorant. She walked firmly back down the stairs.

When she reappeared in the field behind the house, the toasts had already begun. But Susan noticed her immediately. Her sister's eyes were shining triumphantly. It would look inappropriate for Lauren to walk in front of everybody, to take her seat at the end of the table. Lauren just stood there, on the sidelines, watching for at least forty-five minutes, smiling and clapping with everyone else. Then the toasts were over. Some people stayed sitting, waiting to eat, while others rose to the sound of the band.

Lauren watched, with a little thrill, as Chad rose, holding Trisha's hand. As they walked toward the area where people were dancing, Lauren was skirting the crowd, heading in the same direction. She watched them twirl around several times, Trisha constantly smiling, occasionally running her fingers through Chad's hair, and pressing her body against his suggestively. The music started to die down. Another song would begin. Confident that she had given Trisha her chance, Lauren glided toward the couple. When she suddenly appeared in front of them, they both looked startled. Neither one of them had seen her. Lauren looked directly into Trisha's eyes.

"Do you mind if I cut in?" Her glance flickered toward Chad. He was staring at her in confusion. "I have some unfinished business with Chad, Trisha," Lauren continued, glancing imploringly at him. "I just need to talk to him."

Then, before she could say another word, Chad pulled his arm gracefully but determinedly away from Trisha. There was a touch of humor in his voice. His eyes were fully on Lauren.

"Excuse me, Trisha, but Lauren's right. . . . We do have some unfinished business." He seemed to linger over these words. Lauren felt her cheeks burning and instinctively put her hand against one of them.

"Well, okay," Trisha replied, offended.

But Lauren couldn't worry about Trisha's feelings because, a second later, Chad had swept her into his arms.

"So," he said a little menacingly, holding her tightly around the waist. "What do you have to say for yourself?"

Lauren glanced up at him. Her tongue felt tied in clumsy knots. Her cheeks burned hotter than ever. This was the chance she had wanted, the chance she had created. But his firm touch, and the feeling of his body so near to hers, made it impossible for her to think. She slowed down, pulling slightly away from him. Just then she caught sight of Susan and Greg dancing quickly over toward them. Susan stopped, disengaged herself from Greg, and took Chad's hand. But she was looking at Lauren.

"Let's not be greedy, now," she said, little above a whisper.

Chad's reply caught Lauren totally by surprise. He smiled almost condescendingly at Susan, as he looped his arm through Lauren's.

"We're just having a quiet conversation, Susan—that is, if you don't object?"

Susan's glance shot angrily at Chad.

"Why, of course not," she responded with feigned graciousness, all the time her eyes flashing angrily at Lauren.

"Fine, then," Chad said quietly. Then he looked directly at Greg, standing not too far away. "I think the new bride needs to do a lot of dancing, Greg. She seems pretty excited about the day. You'll want to tire her out a bit."

Greg laughed, reaching for Susan's hand. But she pulled it away from him and, after glaring furiously at Chad, stomped off.

Lauren started to walk away. This was getting far too complicated. She rushed through the crowd, not sure if Chad was following her. But as she got out into the open field, she felt a firm hand on her shoulder. A second later he was beside her.

"Why don't you and I go somewhere nice and quiet where we can talk?" He strode very slightly ahead of her.

"I'm not sure," Lauren said hesitantly.

Chad laughed. "Fifteen minutes ago you were so sure you had to talk to me, you risked your life with a real lioness." He stood still, in front of her, blocking her path. She had to look up at him. He reached out, placing his hand on her shoulder again. His voice was low. "And I agreed, against my better judgment, that we should talk.... I think it's the very least you owe me, Lauren. And I don't intend to be put off again."

His face was very serious. All the humor was gone. Lauren looked down at the ground, hesitated a second, then lifted her skirts and started walking.

"There's a place down by the stream," she said nervously. "Why don't we go there?"

"Lead the way," he responded gallantly, motioning her ahead of him.

It was only half a mile from the wedding festivities, but it seemed many worlds away. The stream was surrounded by majestic old willows, whose long draping branches hovered just above the water's surface. Low bushes completely blocked the area from view. It had been one of Lauren's favorite places—her secret place, because Susan never cared to come near it. She was always afraid of messing up her clothes.

Coming here had always helped relax her. But not today. All

she could think about now was how to get this discussion over with as quickly as possible, so she could get back to the reception. She hadn't envisioned talking to him in such a secluded place. She hadn't planned on being alone with him again. She walked quickly toward the water, aware that he was right behind her. She thought she should turn around to face him, but she couldn't bring herself to do it. Finally, she just stood, facing the stream, and began talking. There was no other way.

"I'm sorry about last night. I owe you an apology." The words rushed out of her mouth. She waited a second, somehow expecting him to say "All right," or something. But there was nothing but absolute silence, interrupted only by the quiet sound of his breathing. Her fingers twirled nervously through the yards of ribbon forming a bow at her waist. "I guess I just had a little too much to drink. . . . I'm not much of a drinker . . . a little wine can go a long way. . . ."

"You're lying and you know it!" His clear but harsh voice caught her completely by surprise. She instinctively spun around.

"How dare you say that!" she snapped.

They were standing next to a tree. Chad leaned back against it, a faint, sarcastic smile lighting up his eyes.

"It's not that easy, Lauren," he said, reaching down to pluck a long piece of grass. "I don't know who you're used to leading on, but I can tell you something right now. I don't buy that story about the wine—and we're not leaving here until you tell me the truth."

"I'm telling you the truth," she protested angrily. "I had too much to drink."

"You were throwing yourself at me long before a drop of wine touched your beautiful lips, and you know it. And there's something else." He paused, no longer smiling but still looking her right in the eye. "I've kissed a lot of women, Lauren, and no woman kisses the way you were kissing me just because she's drunk. A woman only kisses like that when she wants something more . . . a lot more."

Lauren stood there in growing agitation. Her cheeks burned;

her heart was beating wildly. She couldn't listen to what he was saying. She couldn't stand there, casually discussing her most intimate soul with . . . with a stranger, someone who didn't care about her at all. His words kept pouring into her ears. She couldn't escape them. All of a sudden she reached out and hit him hard across the face. Then she started running. She hadn't gone more than a few feet when she felt his iron grip closing around her arm. He pulled her to him with a swift gesture.

"I don't have all afternoon, Lauren," he said firmly but gently. "I'm sick of your games. If we're gone too long, people will start to talk." She was silent for a moment, looking down at the grass. He stepped toward her, let go of her hands, and placed his hands on her shoulders. She looked up, startled.

"Okay . . . okay." She stepped back nervously, only to feel his hands tighten. "I'll tell you. . . . I'll tell you right now, I promise."

"Then, start talking," he commanded, still holding her, "and make it fast."

Lauren twisted her fingers nervously. She couldn't look him in the eye.

"It was a bet . . . that's all. Susan and Trisha didn't think I could . . . I could seduce you . . . they didn't think I knew how. . . ."

There was dead silence. Finally Lauren couldn't stand it anymore. She glanced up. He was staring at her with that same amused smile. It infuriated her.

"Please let me go now," she snapped. "I've told you the truth. . . . I'm sorry that it got out of hand . . . that was my fault. . . ."

"But it didn't get out of hand, Lauren. Not at all. You just stopped. Nothing happened."

She took a few steps back. "Well, I had to . . . there were so many people around . . . I didn't realize . . ."

"You knew there were people around when you started."

She stared imploringly at him, her cheeks burning. What could she say? She couldn't tell him the truth. Not a man like Chad. He would laugh at her. And, just being around him, she felt deeply embarrassed about her virginity. He put his hand on the side of her head.

"Did I scare you last night, Lauren?" he said softly, allowing his fingers to sink into the thick, soft mass of hair.

Lauren just shook her head. She didn't trust herself to speak. She didn't want to burst into tears. His hand nuzzled through her hair until it was resting on the back of her neck. His touch sent shivers down her spine. She tried to deny the fact that she wanted to press against him and have him cover her face with kisses and more—yes, she wanted more. She kept her face desperately against his chest.

"I can understand your being nervous," he continued gently, "but I wouldn't hurt you, Lauren. I promise. I'd make you feel things you've never felt before. I want you, Lauren. I want you very much."

She gasped. His words, his closeness—her head was spinning. No one had ever spoken to her like this. Her heart pounding, she slowly looked up. And when her eyes met his, so dark and soft, she knew she couldn't say no. His lips hovered above hers for a second. He was studying her face very seriously.

"Is it okay, Lauren?" he whispered. "Do you want me to kiss you?"

"Yes," she whispered, weak with passion.

His lips met hers with an intensity she could never have imagined possible. They were soft and hard at the same time. Warm and wet. His tongue didn't have to push at her lips. And, when they sank to the ground, she barely noticed that they had even moved.

She lay on her back, unable to keep herself from returning his kisses. Then he pulled away a little. His finger tugged at the wide neckline of her dress, slipping it over her shoulder. She didn't open her eyes. She didn't want to see what he was doing, because she didn't care. Anything he did would be right. She felt his hand smoothing her hair out on the grass, and then she felt his lips against her breast. His kisses streamed along the neckline, lingering on the soft curve that rose above the décolletage.

Lauren pressed herself toward him, moaning, unable to control her breath, which was coming in short panting sounds. He kissed the bare flesh for a long time, arousing her desire with painstaking care, whispering in her ear, telling her how beautiful she was. Every pore in her body ached for his touch, his caress. When his hand slipped behind her and slowly began to unzip her dress, her excitement only increased. She felt no shame. She was glad now that she hadn't given herself to anyone else. The dress started to slip off her shoulders. His masterly hands caressed them, then his lips slipped across her cheek, back to her eager mouth, as though he wanted to postpone the pleasure of looking at her uncovered breasts.

Lauren pulled him to her. His hand slipped down her side, to rest on her hip. Then, once again, his mouth slipped away from hers and found its way down her neck. As it drew closer and closer to her breasts, a sob escaped her, a sob of passion. He stopped and, with infinite gentleness, placed his hand on the side of her head.

"Are you all right, Lauren? I'm not going too fast, am I?"

She shook her head, hard. A tear streamed down her face. It was so beautiful, all of it. She had never felt so beautiful in her entire life. Suddenly his face was just above hers. He brushed the tear away.

"You're not sad, are you?" he said, his voice hoarse with passion.

She shook her head again, as another tear escaped.

"No," she murmured, unable to think at all. "No. I'm happy . . . I'm just so happy that I waited." The words rushed out in a surge of passionate sentiment. He leaned over to kiss her but, just as their mouths were about to meet, he stopped. A curious light came into his eyes.

"You're glad you waited?" he said with quiet amusement.

Suddenly, she felt very self-conscious. What had she admitted?

"I just mean . . . I mean, I'm glad we didn't make love last night . . . that was all I meant, really."

Chad stared into her eyes. There was no way she could avoid looking at him. And as she gazed into his eyes, amusement changed to dead seriousness.

"You haven't been honest with me, Lauren."

She grasped at her dress. It was an inevitable gesture of natural modesty. He was pulling away, into a sitting position.

"I'm not being dishonest, Chad . . . I'm really not."

"I know why you couldn't carry through last night." His eyes fixed her with a ferocious gaze.

She swallowed nervously. "You don't understand."

"Oh, I think I understand all too well, Lauren. The reason Trisha and Susan made that bet is because they knew something I didn't know." Lauren just stared at him, though a tear ran down her cheek. He leaned toward her and placed a firm finger under her chin. "You're a virgin, aren't you?"

More tears flowed down her cheeks. She couldn't avoid his eyes, but she didn't have to talk.

"I should have figured it out," he said finally, taking his finger away. "I can't believe I didn't figure it out. It should have been so obvious. Damn!"

Then he got up and started to walk away. Lauren watched him with mounting anger. Suddenly, all the hurt, humiliation, and frustration burst forth.

"What difference does it make if I'm a virgin?" she shouted at him. "Weren't you having a good time?"

He turned back, his hair disheveled, his face still faintly red, his clothes mussed. He took a couple of steps toward her, then crouched down so they were eye to eye.

"The question is not whether or not I was having a good time. I loved every minute of it. You're a very beautiful . . . a very passionate woman."

"And what's wrong with that?" she asked, sobbing.

Chad laughed, a low reflective laugh.

"There's nothing wrong with that if . . . if you've had some experience with love."

"How am I supposed to get experience?" she cried, dropping her face into her hands.

There was a long silence. Then she felt his hand on her bare shoulder.

"Lauren, I don't want to hurt you. We don't really know each other. . . ."

"But you would go to bed with Trisha, wouldn't you? Or Becky? Why can't you let me decide what I want to do? It's my body. I'm an adult."

Chad sighed very faintly.

"It's not that easy, Lauren. I wouldn't go to bed with Trisha or Becky, but I can't tell you why. I just wouldn't. I would've made love to you . . . because I think you're something special. . . ."

She burst into another fit of tears.

"Please don't say that . . . I don't want to hear you say that. . . ."

"Lauren, too many people could get hurt. Can't you see that? You're not ready for a serious relationship, especially not a first one, and I'm not prepared to settle down. I don't know when or even if I'll ever be ready. Certainly not now. My company is too important to me. For you, it's your education. If I hurt you, it wouldn't be easily forgotten. Our families are related now. It could make all sorts of problems for—"

"For Susan?" she snapped, quickly jumping to her feet.

"Well, sure, for Susan."

"That's just what I thought." Lauren had controlled her tears now. Without looking at Chad, she pulled her dress up over her shoulders and awkwardly managed to zip it up. Then she ran her fingers through her hair.

"Thank you very much for the lovely afternoon, Mr. Bently." She looked him right in the eye. "You've given me something to remember, I assure you."

She started to walk away. A second later he was beside her.

"Leave me alone! Please just leave me alone!" she protested.

"If you'd stop acting like a two-year-old," he said roughly, taking her arm, "you'd realize how damn decent I was to you. I didn't have to stop—and believe me, if it had been anyone else, virgin or no virgin, I wouldn't have."

"I'm flattered!" She didn't bother to look at him. "Now,

would you please use the same enormous self-discipline, since I'm obviously so easy to resist, and let me walk back in peace?"

"I'm afraid I can't do that. Either way, we've been gone long enough to arouse suspicion. If we come back separately, especially with you looking totally miserable, they're liable to think worse of us than if we come back cheerfully—and together."

"I'm in no mood to play games," she snapped. "I'll act however I please."

Chad grabbed her hand and spun her around.

"No, you won't! This day belongs to Susan and Greg—whatever you may happen to feel toward Susan. If you don't pull yourself together and act civilized, I'll take you over my knee in front of the whole crowd."

She stared angrily into his eyes. She knew he wasn't joking. But more importantly, and even more infuriatingly, she knew he was right. They had left together. If they didn't return that way it *would* look suspicious, very suspicious. She allowed him to hold her arm, and walking quickly, they returned in silence.

Not another word passed between them. Susan had gone to get changed, so Lauren was saved from having to tolerate her sister's vitriolic looks—at least temporarily. But when the bride eventually did emerge, dressed elegantly for her honeymoon, she walked directly toward Lauren, who was, by now, standing alone.

"Are you satisfied?" Susan snapped in a low tone only the two of them could hear.

Lauren just stared back. She had already been through so much, she couldn't face another argument with her sister. Susan laughed a low, angry laugh.

"Well," she whispered harshly, "I'm sure it won't make any difference to you, but I want you to know how much you've hurt me, Lauren. You really have. And this was my wedding day. . . ." Susan's voice caught. She paused as though she wanted to say something more, only to be thwarted by tears welling up in her eyes. Flustered, she turned hurriedly and walked away. Seconds later she threw the bouquet.

Trisha and Becky had grouped around Lauren, so Susan had

to throw it in that direction. As the delightful bouquet of white and pink roses with baby's breath sailed through the air, the two older bridesmaids both struggled frantically, positioning themselves to catch it. But somehow they managed to push each other out of the way. Lauren could have caught it, if she had only just held up her hands. The warm sun and the memory of all that had happened that afternoon completely occupied her thoughts. The bouquet fell at her feet.

It was only afterwards, when people began to urge her to pick it up, that she suddenly couldn't bear to be in the crowd another minute. Leaving the bouquet on the ground, she hurried into the house. As she passed through the door, she glimpsed Chad kissing Susan good-bye—he was kissing her on the cheek. There were tears in Susan's eyes. And that was the last time Lauren had seen Chad, to say nothing of the fact that it was also the last time she had seen Susan.

Five years had passed. Five long and rewarding years, which Lauren had seen as the gateway to her future. Graduate school had brought her opportunities, and the experience Chad had said she lacked. Not that Lauren became promiscuous in any sense, but she did form a deep relationship with David Ward, a relationship she had naturally assumed would culminate in marriage. Their interests had been so similar. They were working on their degrees in the same area, organizational psychology. They had even chosen the same co-op program, allowing them to combine the necessary classwork with actual on-the-job experience, working in a huge plastics factory not far from school.

And they had shared the same dream. They both wanted to teach. In an area where teaching jobs were scarce, the best they had hoped for was to get any kind of academic post at all. Yet they had joked, over and over again, about how wonderful it would be to teach together at the private college they had both attended, teaching and living in an old farmhouse in the country, not far from her father's house. It had all seemed too perfect to be real when, in fact, they *were* both offered jobs at the college. That had been only two months before Lauren completed her dissertation. And the very next day her world and her dreams had both fallen apart.

Two months and almost two thousand miles away, even now it brought tears to her eyes. She remembered David's exact words. He wasn't sure. He needed time. Too much was happening in his life. He didn't want to make the mistake of rushing into marriage. In fact he didn't want to see her at all, at least for a while.

All her protests, all her tears, all her reminders to him of the special times they had shared—none of it meant anything. She finally stopped, numbed by the realization that he didn't really care how she felt. His mind was made up. His decision was unilateral and it was also absolute.

Lauren had rushed home that weekend, desperate for the comfort of familiar surroundings, for the security of her father's presence, only to witness him having a heart attack. As she watched him lying unconscious in the intensive care unit, she realized with a tangible pang how old he looked. For the first time in her life she had a sudden dread of loneliness.

Caring for her father, nursing him back to health, had forced her to take stock of her situation. She couldn't allow herself to count on any future with David. No matter how much she might want that, she doubted his reassurances that all he needed was time. She had to go about forming her world, apart from him.

Her father's illness offered her the opportunity to deal with many of their relatives. A lot of them were people she hadn't seen since she'd been a child. A lot of them lived quite far away. But just talking to them made her feel better. And, of course, she had to call Susan several times.

Susan had traveled all over the world with Greg, but now they were settled in Atlanta, where Greg's company had its headquarters. And in five years Susan had not been home once. Lauren had never gone out of her way to communicate with her sister. They exchanged routine Christmas cards and birthday cards, but that was the total extent of their relationship. The incident with Chad hung like a curtain between them. It seemed to be something neither of them would ever forget.

Any number of times Lauren had thought about discussing what had happened. Maybe telling Susan the truth would have eased the situation. Especially when Lauren's relationship with David seemed so stable. But every time she tried to write about Chad, in a letter, or to pick up the phone and tell Susan, at the last minute she couldn't bring herself to do it. The pain Chad had inflicted by his rejection, all her memories of her own immature behavior, were still too clear in her mind. The very thought of it all still made her blush. And it still angered her, too. She would never forget him telling her she was something special. If she'd been so special, why hadn't he ever made any effort to inquire about her? He could have written. There were a lot of things he could have done, even after what had happened. But year after year had gone by, and he had done nothing.

So Lauren's conversations with Susan concerning their father's health were the first occasion the girls had had to communicate regularly in a very long time. And Lauren was amazed to hear the degree of concern Susan felt. Lauren had assumed long ago that Susan didn't really love their father. But his illness seemed to have changed her attitude. And, in addition, Susan seemed truly sorry when she heard that Lauren and David had split up.

So Lauren had felt hopeful when her father suggested that she go down to Atlanta. The trip was not a frivolous one. John McCloud was by now on the mend, but very aware of his own mortality. He had finally decided to draw up a will. Because of tricky details regarding the death of the girls' mother, and her residual estate, he needed Susan's signature on several papers. Susan had been told that his intentions were to leave the farm to Lauren, and to make a financial settlement with her. She hadn't protested a bit, which had come as no surprise. Susan hadn't ever shown any interest in the farm.

But John McCloud had an enormous distrust of the postal service. These papers were vitally important. He didn't want them getting lost! He also knew how badly Lauren needed to get away, and he wanted to mend the rift between his daughters.

The trip had been planned quickly; it had begun dismally, with terrible snow in Connecticut. But now, entering the Atlanta city limits, Lauren felt enormously cheered. It was sunny and at least eighty degrees. She had stopped at a gas station to change into a lightweight skirt and shirt. The bright red piqué had done much to help her feel she was really in another world—a world free of pressures and school, a world free of David.

She picked up the scrap of paper on the seat beside her and consulted the carefully-drawn-up directions. She turned off the freeway onto Peachtree Street, and took it north. Gradually, the shops, car dealerships, and fast-food places disappeared. In their place she now saw elegant old homes, living memories of an age now gone. She allowed her mind to wander, imagining how the city must have looked, a hundred or even a hundred and fifty years earlier. And slowly, as she wound her way through tree-lined residential streets, she came closer and closer to Susan's house.

After a number of confusing turns, which quickly brought her mind back to the present, she pulled up in front of a white clapboard house, surrounded by an old-fashioned screened-in porch and topped by a charming cupola. The front yard was reached by a long stairway leading up from the sidewalk. The yard itself was small but elegantly landscaped, with a magnificent garden already blooming. And everywhere the delicious smell of dogwood filled the air.

Lauren stared, then leaned back to check the address once more. This was definitely Susan's home, but it didn't look at all like the home Lauren was expecting. She had always thought Susan preferred stark, functional modern architecture. But this place was charming—utterly delightful. She felt her spirits rise, just looking at it. After taking a minute to check her makeup in the rearview mirror, she slipped her white bag over her shoulder and stepped out of the car. It was great to be here at last. She was going to enjoy every minute of it. It was going to be the vacation she needed, but it was going to be more than that, too, much more than that. She smiled with a deep happiness and almost hopped up the long flight of wooden stairs.

CHAPTER THREE

"Lauren," Greg exclaimed warmly. "Come on in and let me take a look at you. It's been a long time!"

Lauren hugged him affectionately. Though she hadn't seen her brother-in-law since the wedding, he had a special manner that put everyone at ease.

"It's great to be here," she exclaimed enthusiastically.

Greg looked her over. "You look wonderful. I guess finally being finished with school agrees with you."

"I *am* glad not to be a student anymore," Lauren said lightly, trying to stop herself from thinking about the memories her student days aroused. "But let's not talk about me. Where did you get that gorgeous tan? You look fantastic!"

"South America." Greg grinned. "Lucky me, eh? I've been doing a lot of work down there. As a matter of fact I just got back the other day."

Lauren smiled with approving interest. "I had no idea you ever left the country. Did Susan go with you?"

"Not anymore. Since we bought this house I practically have to pry her away. She says she doesn't like tropical bugs, and I do spend my time in rather exotic places. I try not to be gone for too long at a stretch. I just don't like to leave her alone. Here, let me call her. I'm being rude. She's just out back." He turned toward the kitchen, directly behind them, and called, "Hey, Susan . . . come on in. Lauren's here!"

A second later Susan appeared, carrying pruning clippers. She set them on the counter. She was dressed immaculately in white duck shorts and a simple V-necked shirt of white handkerchief linen. The two girls appraised each other. A pretty smile played around the corners of Susan's mouth. Greg smiled.

"Doesn't she look wonderful, Sue?"

Susan gave her sister a hug, then stepped back, holding her at arm's length. "You do look wonderful," she said with quiet approval. "My little sister has really grown up. It's hard to believe."

"You don't look half bad yourself," Lauren said mischievously. "As a matter of fact, it looks as if you get more beautiful every year."

Susan laughed lightly. "I try my hardest."

"You don't have to try at all, and you know it!" Greg exclaimed, putting his arm affectionately around his wife's shoulders.

Still smiling, Susan pulled slightly away. Not away from his arm, but just far enough away so she wasn't resting against his chest. "The problem with having a husband like Greg is that he doesn't give me any reason to improve. Anything I do is fine with him. I could gain thirty pounds, and I don't think he'd even notice."

"But Susan," Lauren said jovially, "that's a sign of real love. He accepts you just the way you are."

"Believe me," Greg interrupted, "if you gained thirty pounds I'd be thrilled, 'cause I know you'd only do it for one reason."

Susan looked up at Greg; anger flashed beneath her smile. Her eyes moved back to Lauren's face.

"Greg would love me to get pregnant. But I'm not ready. I don't know why he keeps bugging me. There's still lots of time."

Lauren smiled sympathetically. "Children are a lot of responsibility, but I think you'd make a great mother, Sue."

"Maybe later on I would. Right now they'd only get in the way and, besides, Mr. Perfect Father here is never home. I'm not going to raise children alone."

"Honey, you know the second you got pregnant, I'd get a job that kept me here," Greg protested with cheerful vehemence.

Susan made a funny face.

"Oh, let's not talk about all this personal stuff, Greg. We must be boring Lauren to death. Go and get her bags and I'll fix her something cool to drink. She must be tired, after that long drive."

The two sisters wandered toward the kitchen, passing through the living room and dining room on the way.

"The house is gorgeous," Lauren remarked, noticing the elegant high ceilings and the beautifully polished hardwood floors, covered with Oriental rugs. "It's really not at all what I expected."

Susan laughed lightly. "In some ways I guess it wasn't what I expected, either. But I wanted a lot of room, and short of spending a fortune, you just can't get this kind of spaciousness in modern homes."

"How many bedrooms do you have?"

"Six, if you count the little cupola." Susan paused, registering her sister's shocked expression. "You think I'm crazy, don't you?"

"Well, either that or you're planning on having a large family."

"It's really not that many rooms, if you figure it out." They reached the kitchen, which was huge; there seemed to be hundreds of cupboards around the periphery. On one side of the main room was a huge cooking area, around which hung a wide assortment of copper pans. Lauren admired the beautifully tiled floor, then shifted her gaze to the magnificent round oak table that monopolized the other half of the floor space.

"You could feed an army in here," she remarked, amazed.

"I know it must seem extravagant to you, but try to remember that I lived out of a suitcase, in hotel rooms, for three and a half years. I had to have some space."

"I guess so," Lauren admitted. Susan poured them glasses of iced tea. "So tell me what you do with all those bedrooms. I interrupted you."

They sat down at the oak table, facing each other. "Well, let's see. Of course, we have the master bedroom, then a guest room, Greg uses one room as a study, I use one room as a sewing room, then there's Chad's room, and one tiny bedroom we call a den."

Lauren stared at her sister in disbelief, but Susan's face didn't seem to register any surprise.

"So that's it," Susan concluded matter of factly. "As you can see, we use every inch of space."

Lauren sat quietly, trying to absorb what she had just heard. Finally, she cleared her head enough to ask a question.

"Does Chad visit here often?" She tried to sound as confident as possible, as if she were asking for no other reason than passing curiosity.

Susan didn't hesitate. "Quite a lot. His business has expanded tremendously. He opened an office here three years ago." She smiled sweetly. "That's one of the reasons we settled here. He and Greg are very close. And, to tell you the honest truth, I got sick of staying alone when Greg's out of town. So whenever Chad has business here, he stays in the house. You'll see him later on."

"You mean he's staying in the house now?" Lauren asked, feeling a growing sense of agitation.

"Sure," Susan answered casually. "He's downtown now, but he'll be back this evening. You're not upset that you're not the only guest, are you? He's not really a guest, after all. He's family. But then, so are you," she noted with casual cheerfulness.

"No, really, it's fine. . . ." Lauren's voice trailed off. "I just wish I'd known. That's all."

"Well, I'm sorry I didn't say anything. I just didn't think it was a big deal."

Lauren forced herself to smile, though her thoughts were on other things. "It isn't a big deal. It's just that . . ." She paused and stared rather nervously at Susan, unsure about whether or not to speak. The line of her mouth tightened with resolve. Her voice was low but steady. "I'm a little surprised you didn't mention it, because I thought you were angry at me all these years about what happened at your wedding."

Susan's eyes widened with ever-increasing amusement. Then she burst out laughing. "You've *got* to be kidding! Do you still think about that?"

Lauren suddenly felt her anger begin to grow. There was

something mocking in Susan's tone that had always bothered her. But she forced herself to stay calm. There was no need to let herself get upset about something so small. After all, one of her reasons for coming was to renew her relationship with Susan. She couldn't let Chad get in the way of that.

"Hardly at all. It happened so long ago I can't really remember it."

A wicked little smile played on the corners of Susan's mouth. "Well, don't give it a moment's thought on my account. I'm a big girl and I can take care of myself. And as for Chad, you needn't worry about him."

"Oh, I wasn't," Lauren quickly interposed.

"I just mean," Susan went on, "that I'm sure he doesn't remember that time at all. He's been very busy with his company. And, truthfully, he has more women friends than I can keep track of. He's the same Chad Bently!"

As Susan finished speaking, Greg appeared at the door. Lauren felt relieved by the distraction.

"Lauren," he pronounced with mock formality, "your bags have been deposited in your room. May I show you where you'll be staying?"

"It would be my pleasure," Lauren said cheerfully. She stood up and jokingly offered him her hand.

Susan stood by the back door. "Take some time to freshen up, sis. I'll just go out and finish pruning the lilac bush."

They headed toward the staircase, wide old oak steps and a decadently ornate bannister. With typical Greg-boyishness he took the stairs two at a time. Lauren laughed at his extraordinary energy. At the top he turned and faced her.

"I'm really glad to see you," he declared with a smile on his face but a deep sincerity in his voice.

She smiled back, feeling just a little embarrassed. "Well, you know I'm happy to be here."

"I've been a little concerned about Susan lately," he continued, almost as though he hadn't heard what she said.

"Is there anything the matter? She looks wonderful."

They walked along the broad hall until they reached a small

door. He paused there and rubbed the back of his neck. A perplexed expression came over his face, then he laughed nervously. "It's probably nothing. I'm the biggest worrywart to come along in years."

"Has she said anything to make you worry?" she asked with growing concern.

"No, nothing at all. It's just a feeling I get. I think maybe she's homesick, but I can't talk her into visiting your father." He leaned back against the wall and a look of anxiety spread over his face. He seemed to be deciding whether or not to go on. When he did speak, his voice sounded a little shaky. "And sometimes, I'm not too sure she's happy with me."

His eyes met hers and she tried not to betray the real shock she felt.

"I understand the part about home," she said consolingly. "I know Dad would love to see her. But I'm sure she's happy with you. You're a wonderful husband, Greg. How can you doubt that?"

Greg smiled and seemed more relaxed. "Hey, listen, I didn't mean to lay all of this stuff on you. Forget what I said. Just concentrate on having a good time. That's sure to help Susan. Did she tell you Chad is here?"

"She mentioned it," Lauren answered, a little shaken by the sudden change of topic.

"You met him at the wedding, didn't you?"

She only nodded. Greg smiled.

"I remember he was pretty much taken with you, back then."

"That was a long time ago."

"Almost five years, exactly," he mused, opening the door and starting up a narrow flight of stairs. "Now, wait till you see this!" he exclaimed as they emerged into the room at the top.

She looked around in amazement. "This is beautiful! We were so caught up in conversation, I had no idea we were heading up here. I didn't stop to think. I love it."

"That's exactly what Susan said." He laughed. "If you feel in the mood to sketch, this is the place." His arm gestured to include the panoramic view provided by the nearly complete circle of windows.

Lauren stared out, enraptured by her surroundings. If anything could take her mind off her worries, this was it. The quality of light in the room was dazzling; her mind was flooded with ideas for watercolors. Beneath her gaze lay a gorgeous picture of rich abundant foliage, interrupted by the graceful constructions of another age. The warm air and the brilliant sun helped to conjure up pictures of carriages, mammies, bustles, and elegance. She turned to face Greg.

"This is spectacular," she exclaimed joyfully. "But I warn you, you may have to drag me down, to get me away from this view. If this were the only sight I saw in my visit, it would be enough."

"Then the least I can do is leave you to your enjoyment. The bathroom is to your right, at the bottom of the stairs. Relax and prepare for dinner. Susan's a great cook."

Lauren smiled warmly at her brother-in-law. "Thanks a lot, Greg. And believe me, I hope my visit does help Susan feel better."

"Don't worry about it. There's probably no problem at all."

When she heard the door close at the bottom of the stairs, Lauren turned her attention to her suitcase. She opened it, looked at the neatly packed clothing for a minute, then sank down on the bed. A mixture of feelings crowded her mind. The conversation with Greg filled her with a strange nagging feeling about Susan. Not that Susan hadn't been welcoming and nice, it was just that . . . Lauren drew a blank. There was something about her sister she didn't understand. The whole casual way in which she had mentioned Chad being there, for example.

And yet, if Susan really didn't feel bothered by the situation, that was a good sign. Certainly, if her sister could put the past behind her, Lauren could do the same. And she had every intention of doing so. She felt much better about being in Atlanta than she had realized she would. She wasn't going to allow Chad's presence to change that. This was her vacation! And it had been hard earned. It shouldn't be too hard to avoid him, after all. And the times when she did have to see him, well, she had gained enough experience to know how to put a man off. Especially an arrogant man. In fact, as she thought about it, she realized it would be a pleasure to behave with the cool assurance she knew she had mastered.

Her eyes roamed around the room with a new curiosity. She had been so captivated with what lay beyond the walls, she had barely noticed what was inside them. The room was simply decorated. The carpeting was pale cream. Against the one small wall that was not a window stood a discreet pine dresser, stripped to its natural color and polished to a high luster. It matched the pine trim on the inside of each window. Several large pots with elegant ferns and philodendrons added a lively dash of color. And, in the middle of the room, stood the bed with its beautiful brass frame. It was a double bed and the sun seemed to glint off the metal, making it look still larger. She sighed. She had wanted a brass bed for a long time, but she had always associated it with a loving relationship. She and David had talked about buying one, someday. It seemed odd that she would sleep in one now, alone. She quickly repressed the thought.

It was almost four thirty and she wanted to take a long languorous bath, to help relax her before dinner. If she was going to see Chad, she wanted to have the upper hand. She unpacked her things, arranging them hastily in the empty drawers. Then she slipped out of her skirt and shirt and into her robe, took some beautiful herbal bath salts, and descended to the bathroom. Minutes later she was immersed in a deliciously hot tub.

By six she was dressed again, in a cool cotton knit wrap dress. Her hair was just beginning to dry; its gold highlights seemed richer still, in the setting sun shining into her room. She went downstairs, feeling confident and ready to face anyone.

But there was no one to face. Susan and Greg were her only dinner companions. From Susan's steadfast silence about Chad, Lauren could only deduce that he had made other plans and had perhaps offended Susan in the process.

And, aside from that, the atmosphere in the dining room was

far from cordial. Susan seemed distracted and tense and just generally inattentive to Greg. Lauren kept remembering what he had told her. If this went on constantly, she could easily understand how he got the impression his wife didn't much care for him.

Finally, around nine thirty, when it was very obvious that there was no point waiting for Chad to return, Lauren excused herself for the night. But though she had driven practically thirty hours straight, it wasn't really fatigue that made her seek the solitude of her room. It wasn't even the tension between Susan and Greg, though that bothered her enormously. It was the knowledge that Chad must have known she was coming and had obviously not cared enough even to greet her courteously.

As she stretched out between the cool sheets, she felt increasingly angry. She had thought she was long since over the crazy infatuation she had felt, once, a long time ago, for her sister's brother-in-law. But now all the hurt he had caused her was back in force. She could feel her cheeks burning in the moonlight radiating throughout the room. Finally, she couldn't stand it anymore. There was only one way she could deal with this situation. She had been naive to think they would both be capable of behaving like adults. His arrogant discourteousness made that impossible. She would simply have to treat him exactly the way he was treating her—with total indifference.

The thought calmed her, in an odd way. She drifted off to sleep, feeling more confident.

Morning came quickly. Lauren glanced at the clock, fully expecting it to be little more than six o'clock A.M. She sat up with a start when she saw that the hands read ten thirty. She had slept at least twelve hours.

She slipped into a pair of navy shorts and a white shirt. Then she padded downstairs in her bare feet. The house seemed absolutely silent. When she reached the kitchen, she found a note on the table.

* * *

Dear Lauren,

   I didn't want to wake you. I've gone to my art class. Do whatever you like. I'll see you between noon and one.

   Susan

She took a pear from the bowl on the table. It had been very considerate of Susan not to wake her—very considerate indeed. Because it also meant she hadn't had to see Chad that morning. That would surely give him a clue about her feelings. He might not have seen fit to come home the evening before but, on the other hand, it was clear she wasn't so desperate to see him that she jumped up earlier than usual.

She smiled to herself and wandered out into the backyard. The sun was so bright, the sky was so blue. This was her vacation. She stretched out on a chaise, unbuttoning her shirt much lower than usual. Encircled by trees, the yard was extremely private. And there was no one at home. She would soak up a few rays before returning to her room to sketch.

She settled down quickly, to the sound of bees buzzing and birds chirping. But she hadn't been there long before her morning reverie was interrupted by a pitiful sound. It was the most elongated "meoow" Lauren had heard in a long time. At first she didn't respond. But when she heard it a second and third time, in rapid succession, she realized she was in for a concert unless she did something.

It wasn't long before she spotted the problem—the small problem. Sitting up in the chaise, she could see a tiny marmalade kitten out on the bough of a huge old elm. And he was looking right at her.

She laughed as she stood up.

"Just a second," she called to her distressed visitor.

It had been some time since Lauren climbed a tree, but it was certainly not a skill she had forgotten. She quickly spotted a small table beside the garage. She panted a little as she carried it over to the tree. Thank God it was there. The tree was so big she'd need something to help her reach the lowest branch, the one just beneath where the kitten was stranded.

As she stood on the shaky table, figuring out her safest toe hold, her only regret was that she hadn't bothered to wear her tennis shoes. They would have given her more traction. But she wasn't about to go back. She had climbed trees in her bare feet before. She could do it now.

She located a large lump on the bark. It looked like some kind of fungal growth. But it was solid, so she placed her left foot on it and, springing just a little, was able to grab hold of the branch. She dexterously hoisted herself up, straddling it for stability. After some coaxing the kitten moved nervously toward her. When he stood directly above her, on the next branch, she was able to scoop him into her arms. And that was when the trouble began.

Getting down with a kitten in her arms was not going to be nearly as easy as getting up without one. She cursed, as her foot strained to reach a secure place on the trunk. She was at least ten feet up. As a child she probably would have jumped. But she'd been much more compact, then—she hadn't had nice long legs to break. As the minutes dragged on, her arms began to tire. She tried to put the kitten back down on the branch. Maybe she could get down herself, then find a ladder and come back up. But he was having none of it. Claws out, he clung to her, scratching her chest.

In desperation she reached farther down with her foot. Finding something beneath it, she assumed it was the toe hold she had used to climb up. She lowered her weight. It was only as she sighed with relief, feeling she was almost safe, that a sudden terror filled her. Whatever was holding her started to break away from the tree. She tried desperately to regain her balance, to no avail. She was falling, at a dizzying, frantic speed. Her mind started to go blank, as she anticipated hitting the ground. But just before she blacked out completely, she realized she had landed in someone's arms. And together she and her rescuer tumbled over onto the grass.

For a second she lay absolutely still, too shocked and relieved to move. The kitten scampered away. Then curiosity got the better of her. Who was her silent rescuer? He hadn't said a word. Maybe the fall had hurt him. She scrambled to her knees.

"That was quite a little performance you put on." The familiar voice rang in her ears. She was face to face with Chad Bently, five years older, but looking exactly the same, regarding her with his perpetually amused expression.

Why did it have to be him, she swore to herself? Why couldn't it have been the plumber, or at least someone unobnoxious?

"I suppose I'm now eternally indebted to you, for saving my life," she finally said, controlling her sarcasm only slightly.

Chad laughed, leaning back on the grass. "Is that any way to greet an old friend, Lauren?"

She stared at him, the faintest trace of a smile touching the corners of her mouth. "Friend?" she finally said rather dubiously. "I don't really think that word applies to our brief relationship."

"It may have been brief, as you say." Chad smiled easily, pushing himself back into a sitting position. "But it was certainly memorable." He reached out and ran a finger down her bare arm. Lauren pulled coolly away.

"So memorable, in fact, that you made every effort to stay in touch with me?"

A shadow of uncertainty passed over his eyes. Lauren rose to her feet.

"I'll talk to you later, Chad. I'd like to clean up a bit. Excuse me."

She started walking toward the house. It wasn't until she had reached the door that she felt a hand on her shoulder. She glanced sharply back.

"You look fine, Lauren . . . a bit uncomfortable, but beautiful." He paused. "I think you're more beautiful than ever."

She just glared at him. His hand slipped down her arm to her hand. She tried to pull it away. He was scrutinizing her fingers—most especially her wedding-ring finger. She looked down at it, too, to hide her red cheeks.

"Please, Chad." Her voice was anxious but quiet.

"We haven't seen each other in five years," he remarked with gentle humor. "Are you still angry at me?"

Her eyes met his. She studied his handsome face for several seconds, then firmly shook her head.

"No," she said slowly. "That's all very much in the past. A lot of other things—"

"So I heard," he interrupted. "You've had all your schooling ... and then Susan told me you had a boyfriend—something very serious, apparently. . . ." His voice trailed off. His eyes moved back to her hand.

Lauren laughed weakly—anything to lighten the effect he was having, standing so close to her.

"I had no idea Susan was in the habit of discussing me."

"She isn't," Chad said quietly, looking her right in the eye. "I asked."

She stared at him, dumbfounded. Then she dropped her gaze to the porch. Her initial confusion was quickly replaced by irritation.

"Well, I'm deeply touched that I happened to cross your mind—"

"I've thought about you a lot, Lauren," he interrupted her again. "I didn't want to interfere—"

"Would it have been interfering with anything but your rampant social life if you'd managed to come home for dinner last night, to greet me?" Her eyes flashed angrily. She pulled her hand firmly away from his. "Words aren't everything, you know, Chad." She had reached for the door as she spoke.

"If words aren't everything, Lauren, how about a kiss hello?" Chad said softly, moving closer to take her in his arms.

For a few brief seconds she looked into his dark shimmering eyes. For a few brief seconds she tried to deny the yearning for him that had been slowly welling up inside. But when his smooth, wet lips crushed hers and when his arms encircled her, drawing her closer and closer till her breasts pressed against his hard, muscular chest, there could be no denying the eagerness with which her whole body responded—just as she had five years ago, with an intensity of feeling she hadn't known since then.

A thousand confused thoughts fought with her growing desire, all to no avail. Her hands, which had tried hard to push him away, remained on his chest, unresisting. Then slowly they began to move, massaging the taut flesh beneath the thin shirt, gradually working their way up until they clasped behind his neck. Lauren and Chad stood wrapped in this silent but passionate reunion, all time obliterated. When their lips finally did part, Lauren had to stifle the sudden sense of deprivation. She looked up into his dark eyes, uncertainly.

"That was some hello. . . ." she began, before he put his finger against her lips. He was smiling with all the contentment of the cat who'd just got the cream.

"I thought so," he said calmly. "I had to get through to you somehow—our talks always seem to turn into arguments. And I hope you're not going to try to convince me you didn't enjoy that?"

"I'm not going to try to convince you of anything," she replied with quiet determination, though her whole body felt hot and flushed. As she felt her cheeks start to color, she turned to go into the house. He followed, laughing a low subtle laugh.

"So you did enjoy it?"

She was heading toward the stairs, annoyed to find he could easily keep up with her.

"Don't flatter yourself, Chad." She glanced back at him, smiling.

"We'll have to see about that . . . in the next three weeks," he replied in a low, seductive voice.

He spoke with such finality and such assurance that even though she had one foot on the stairs and could have been away from him in a matter of seconds, she stopped dead in her tracks, turning to face him.

"Chad Bently, I'm here to visit with my sister, not you. Please don't make any mistake about that. Just leave me alone."

He placed his hand on the bannister, moving a little closer. His eyes twinkled appreciatively at the wide-open neckline of her shirt.

"I'm not sure I'm going to be able to." His voice was quiet but determined.

She smiled reassuringly. "I don't think it should be a problem. You didn't have any trouble five years ago. You haven't had any trouble since then."

"There were other considerations then, Lauren . . . and I haven't seen you in quite a while."

"I'll try to make sure you don't see too much of me now."

"We'll have to see each other at least once a day, at dinner."

"As I understand it," she responded, looking straight at him, "you come and go as you please. I'm sure there'll be many evenings when you'll be busy. Every girl in Atlanta must be fighting to go out with you."

"You drive a hard bargain, Lauren. But this time you've won." He laughed.

She smiled perfunctorily. "I'm glad I've managed to convince you—"

"Well, I really was almost convinced," he interrupted, shaking his head, "but then I remembered how upset you were that I didn't come home to greet you last night, and my instinct told me—"

Lauren just stared at him, studying every line on his face.

"—that this is your way of saying you want to see more of me," he concluded. "So I'll just have to be sure I make myself more available."

Lauren laughed, starting up the stairs. "Do what you like, Chad. Hang around as much as you like. I'm perfectly capable of resisting you. If you don't believe that—"

"There's only one thing I believe, Lauren, and that's what your kisses tell me."

She stopped at the top of the stairs. "You are the most insufferable man I have ever met!"

"At least I've distinguished myself in some way. Well, listen. I'd love to continue our charming conversation, but I've got to be going. I just came back to pick up some papers. See you at dinner." He winked, then smiled and headed toward the door.

Lauren cursed. She might have hurled something at him if he

hadn't slipped out the door before she had the chance. God damn him, she thought. She had come down here to get away from tensions. Instead, she'd walked into more than she could stand. Well, if he wouldn't be gone for dinner, she would. There must be plenty of sights she could go to see! And she would make a habit of it. She probably wouldn't have to be gone too many nights before she succeeded in communicating her message.

She hurried upstairs. Sketching always calmed her down. She'd be sure to relax. She had to relax. It was almost noon. Susan would be home soon. She took several deep breaths and sank down on the bed, with her pad and pencil. But the lines came with great difficulty. Concentration seemed impossible. And, when she finally heard the front door open and close, she was relieved at the prospect of some distraction. She ran down.

"Hi, there," she called from the stairs.

Susan looked up, smiling. "Hi. Are you just getting up?"

"No, I've been up since ten thirty," Lauren said with forced cheerfulness. "Thanks for letting me sleep in."

Susan headed for the kitchen. Lauren followed.

"I had a great class," Susan said a little breathlessly. "How was your morning?"

Lauren hesitated. "Uneventful," she finally said, quietly.

"Oh, really?" Susan said facing her. "Chad said he was going to stop back to see you. Didn't he show up?"

Lauren bit her lip. That man was impossible! So he had planned that whole thing. And she could read the uneasiness in Susan's eyes.

"Well, he did stop by, but it was very quick. He just wanted to say he'd be home for dinner tonight."

Susan smiled tightly, looking away from Lauren. "It was certainly nice of him to tell us his plans, for a change."

"Is he in the habit of just not showing up, even when he's said he would?" Lauren inquired, hiding the true extent of her interest.

"All the time," Susan replied. But she seemed very nervous. She opened the refrigerator. "Let's have a quick lunch, then I'll take you to the museum."

"Sounds wonderful. I'll bet there are a lot of interesting sights to visit here. I want to be sure I see absolutely everything."

Susan laughed. "Don't be silly, Lauren. If you try to do that, you won't have a moment's rest."

"Well, actually, I'm not all that tired. I think what I need is activity—but something different from what I usually do."

Susan handed her a bowl of tunafish and a lemon. She seemed very thoughtful.

"If that's what you feel like, Lauren, it's fine with me." She paused. "It's just that I'm pretty busy myself during the day—classes and such—you'd probably have to do a lot of it on your own."

"That's fine! Give me a map of the city and I won't have any problems."

Susan smiled with satisfaction. "Actually, I'm kind of glad that's your attitude. Greg and Chad are usually so busy, I'm sure they wouldn't have time to show you around, either. This way they won't feel embarrassed about not being able to do it."

"I wouldn't want to put anyone out, believe me. I feel like I need to do a lot—just to keep my mind off things."

"I understand completely," Susan agreed.

"Oh, by the way, why don't I get those papers Dad needed you to sign? We could get it out of the way. Then I wouldn't have to think about it again."

"Oh," Susan said hesitantly. "Don't rush off now. I'll look at them later. I'm sure we won't forget."

Lauren felt vaguely uncomfortable, but she dismissed it as nothing more than a holdover of her anxieties about Chad. But she really had nothing to worry about. Susan seemed very pleased. Everything would be well taken care of. Satisfied, she put everything but lunch out of her mind. And the meal was quiet but cordial. It wasn't until they were returning from the museum that the conversation drifted back to Chad. The drive home had seemed longer, because of the heat. They were stopped at a red light.

"Oh, by the way, Lauren, since Chad's coming home for dinner, I have a word of warning for you."

Lauren laughed, embarrassed. Susan sounded casual, and yet Lauren could tell there was a strong undercurrent of seriousness.

"Oh, I don't think you need to warn me, Susan. I learned my lesson five years ago."

Susan hesitated. "Well, you *are* very smart, Lauren. I'm sure I don't need to warn you. But women get very forgetful when they're around Chad. It's really nothing at all. I just think you should know you can't believe everything he says."

"Is that all?" Lauren asked incredulously.

"That's it," Susan responded with relief.

"Have no worries. I think my limited experience has taught me to be skeptical of everything any man says. Any man except our father, that is."

"Of course," Susan responded quietly.

Minutes later they pulled into the driveway.

"Our beautiful guest sees fit to bestow her charming presence on us," Greg exclaimed, as Lauren entered the living room. She was dressed in a simple red cotton sundress, neatly pintucked to the waist, emphasizing the curve of her bust. The spaghetti straps flattered her fine-boned shoulders and elegant neck. Greg patted the chair next to his. She managed to sit down without having to look Chad in the eye.

"So," Greg continued enthusiastically, "this must be the first time you've seen Chad in five years. What do you think?"

Lauren's eyes flickered toward Chad, but she never had the chance to respond.

"No, it isn't, Greg." Chad smiled fully at Lauren. "I forgot some papers this morning. I had to come back—and as luck would have it, I was just in time."

"In time for what?" Greg remarked amusedly, just as Susan returned to the room, carrying a tray of cocktails. She glanced at her husband with alarm, as though she understood exactly what he was talking about. Lauren rose, taking the tray from Susan. She walked right over to Chad.

"Just in time to see me look my worst." She stared at him with consternation, and long enough and hard enough for him to take

61

the Scotch and water from the tray. Then she swept away, smiling at Greg and Susan. "I'd been up only a few minutes. I'm afraid Chad must think my hair normally looks like a mop—it was a rather embarrassing way to renew a friendship." She had finished serving the drinks. She sat down gracefully and sipped at her frosty gin and tonic. A determined smile remained on her lips. "Luckily, he had the decency not to overdo his welcome."

Chad laughed. "I must say your appearance now certainly makes that description you gave of yourself this morning sound ... false?"

"As a matter of fact," Lauren replied, "your showing up so 'unexpectedly' almost struck me as planned." Lauren glanced at Susan. To her surprise, her older sister was wearing an amused expression. But Susan said nothing.

"If I didn't know better," Greg interposed, "I'd say you two weren't overly fond of each other."

"Quite the contrary." Chad smiled warmly at Lauren. For a second the smile totally vanished from her face. What was he going to say? Then she composed herself again.

"Yes," she concurred, "not having to see someone for five whole years can do wonders for the relationship—"

"I couldn't agree more," Chad interrupted cheerfully. "Lauren is more beautiful than ever." He hesitated just long enough to savor the anger flashing in her eyes. "Not to change the subject," he continued, "but I have a rather interesting proposal to make to our guest. I'm in a bit of a fix down at the office. Two days ago my personnel director told me she was leaving. As it happens, I'm in the middle of negotiating a difficult but very lucrative contract. I'm not going to have time to hire someone to replace her. What with union regulations, and all the other details involved in handling employees with such varied backgrounds, I really can't afford to be without someone who can fill in, as well as help me look for a replacement."

Lauren just stared at him, noticing the wicked twinkle in his eyes. For the first time Susan looked interested in the conversation. She had leaned forward in her chair.

"What are you suggesting?" She laughed nervously.

"Well, I was thinking that Lauren might like to help out—all in the family, of course. From what Greg has told me, she's uniquely qualified."

"But this is her vacation," Susan protested, glancing at Lauren with real concern. "Aren't you falling into your old habit of asking a lot of other people, Chad?"

Lauren was sure there was something else passing between Chad and Susan. They didn't seem to be talking about what they were talking about.

"Susan's right," Lauren remarked to hide her discomfort. The fact that Chad would even suggest such a thing was totally inappropriate. There was more to this, but what? "This *is* my vacation. I came down here to relax. I don't want to get into the whirlwind of a new job—even if it would be only for a few weeks. I need to rest. I start teaching in the fall."

Chad glanced at Greg confusedly.

"Greg," he said seriously, "didn't you tell me, just before Lauren came down, that she had mentioned she wanted to stay busy—no, I think you said she felt she 'needed' to stay busy?"

Greg shrugged. "That's what Susan told me. She said Lauren was planning to see every sight in Atlanta."

"That's something entirely different from working," Susan protested again. "Sightseeing is—relaxing."

"Oh, I don't think so," Chad said matter-of-factly. "Especially not when you go all by yourself."

"I couldn't agree more," Greg remarked. "As a matter of fact, I think it's totally inappropriate for Lauren to be looking around Atlanta on her own."

"But apparently you and Chad are too busy to go with me—and so is Susan," Lauren stated firmly. "I'd be silly not to look around myself. I'm certainly not afraid."

"I'm sure you're not, Lauren." Chad smiled beatifically. "But it's much more fun going with someone—and, as a matter of fact, since I'd be asking so much of you, I'd be perfectly prepared to steal some time to show you around myself."

"I can't imagine how you could suggest . . ." Lauren began exasperatedly.

"Really, Chad." Susan rose anxiously, heading for the door to the kitchen. "Why don't we have dinner? I don't think we should discuss this crazy idea one second longer."

Greg laughed as they took their places at the table.

"I don't know what's with you girls! I think Chad has made a very reasonable, not to say generous, offer. Even if you look at the job offer as simply a way to get some solid experience. Lauren, really. I can tell you're very interested in your work. How can you turn this down? And, on top of that, you'd even have someone to escort you all around Atlanta. Believe me, he knows the city much better than Susan or me."

"I'm sure he does," Lauren remarked moodily, stabbing at her salad.

"In fact," Chad said cheerfully, "I've already planned our itinerary. I'll make sure you dine in every elegant restaurant in the city—at my expense, of course. I'd see escorting you around, every evening, as the least I could do to repay you for all the help you're going to be."

Susan lowered her fork to her plate. Her eyes riveted anxiously on Chad.

"Aren't you presuming a lot, Chad? Lauren hasn't by any means agreed to go along with this haywire idea of yours. She's much too sensible to waste her vacation on you."

"I can't see why not, Susan. You're never around—you're so busy with classes and such. Of course," Chad said slowly, "there is the chance that she might say no. But quite frankly, I can imagine only two reasons for that. First of all, she might be extremely ungrateful, and for some obscure reason not want me to show her around or"—he paused, looking at Lauren with real amusement—"and I don't mean to indicate that the first reason wouldn't be extremely ungracious. But secondly, she might not feel qualified. A lot of times people go into teaching because they can't take the give and take of the marketplace—they're not skilled enough. I would certainly understand if Lauren admitted that. Anybody would."

Lauren gritted her teeth. His efforts to insult her wouldn't provoke her to accept the offer—but there were other things that might. Maybe up till now she had indeed been too narrow-minded. Maybe she was overlooking the perfect way to put Chad Bently in his place, once and for all. She had complete confidence in her ability to handle him. That wasn't even an issue. If she could do that, why did she have to worry about working with him?

And there was another consideration. It was true she had had on-the-job experience at the plastics factory, but once she started teaching it would be a long time before she would be out in the marketplace again. Chad was in fact offering her a golden opportunity to test her skills, to gain some invaluable experience. After three or four weeks she would return home not only more experienced but also having proved to Chad—and yes, to herself—that he really meant nothing to her. She looked up, smiling directly at him.

"I think you're absolutely right, Chad. It would be ungrateful of me to turn down your generous offer. And there's a lot to be gained from the work situation."

"Great!" Greg exclaimed.

"Lauren," Susan said anxiously, "I can't believe you're going along with this snowball job. You're old enough to realize he's just tricked you into helping him. What do you get out of it, aside from the fact that you've given away your vacation?"

"It's okay, Susan," Lauren said quietly. "I know what I'm doing." Her gaze shifted to Chad. "I think there's a lot to be gained—a lot. And there's also a principle at issue. That's how I see it."

"I knew that was how you'd see it." Chad's quiet voice was just a bit smug. Lauren only smiled.

The rest of the meal passed with very casual conversation. Susan said nothing. Her pretty face was clouded with misgivings. Lauren felt doubly bad because she knew she couldn't really tell Susan why she had changed her mind. But maybe when it was all over—maybe then.

It was ten o'clock when they finally left the table. Lauren excused herself.

"You like to go to bed pretty early," Chad remarked.

65

Lauren smiled. "I want to be very fresh for the job. I assume I start tomorrow?"

"The sooner the better," he said.

"I couldn't agree more," Lauren concurred. Then she headed off, feeling cheerful, even buoyant. Now that it was settled, she could hardly wait to start. Oh, would she show Mr. Know-It-All Bently a thing or two! She'd not only beat him at his own game, and hands-down easily, but she'd introduce him to some tricks of the trade that he'd never known existed. She wasn't giving up a vacation, she was gaining something even better—a thorough, complete, and very final revenge.

CHAPTER FOUR

Lauren awoke the next morning, both refreshed and excited. She didn't have too much with her that would be appropriate business wear, but she had enough to get by until she had the opportunity to shop. Susan had mentioned any number of boutiques the other day. She'd take a lunch hour or two and explore.

Today, she slipped into a marine-blue linen skirt and matching boat-necked top. She cinched her waist with a deep fuchsia sash and headed down the stairs. Susan greeted her, still floating around the kitchen in a gorgeous pale pink robe.

"Oh, hi!" she said uncomfortably. "I can't get used to the fact that you're going to be a working girl."

"Neither can I," laughed Lauren. "Isn't Chad up yet?" she remarked, looking around the room.

"Who are you kidding? He leaves at six thirty. He left a note for you." Susan twirled around, pointing at the kitchen table. Her expression was still serious, even troubled. Lauren snatched up the single folded piece of white paper.

"Oh, good, he left instructions on how to get there. I sure hope he doesn't want me to get up early enough to leave at six thirty. That's where I draw the line."

"Do you want coffee?" Susan interrupted.

"Thanks, Susan."

But when Susan handed her the steaming mug and quickly turned away, Lauren set Chad's note down.

"I'm sorry, Susan. I'm being rude. Have you had breakfast yet?"

Susan shrugged. "I never eat breakfast."

"Well, at least join me for a cup of coffee."

Susan headed for the door of the kitchen. "Not this morning, Lauren. I've got too much to do."

"Susan?" Lauren called after her sister. Susan stopped but didn't turn to face her. Lauren continued. "Susan, I hope I haven't offended you in any way by accepting Chad's offer."

"No . . . no, you haven't," Susan replied, after a brief pause. "It's just that you've seemed very upset since last evening."

"You're old enough to handle the situation, Lauren. Just keep in mind what I told you. I've known Chad a lot longer than you have . . . we've lived in close quarters." She hesitated a second. "Never mind, really. It's nothing. . . ." Her voice trailed off. Lauren stood watching her, feeling unusually awkward. She had to say something to ease Susan's mind.

"I'll be okay, Susan," she finally said. "It's really just a matter of principle—that's all. I'll tell you about it sometime."

Susan laughed very slightly. "Well, no big deal, eh? I've got to go upstairs and dress. I'll see you this evening."

"Sure," Lauren replied quietly, as Susan started up the stairs. She stood there a second longer, then took a deep breath and returned to the table. The coffee was delicious—unusually satisfying. As she drank it, she reviewed the directions once again. She had a real feeling of pleasure. It was good that they weren't driving to work together. Maybe her acceptance had intimidated him more than he showed. If so, that was a stroke of luck for her. This way she'd have her own car, she'd come and go as she pleased. Mostly go, she thought. Yes, there was no reason why she couldn't skip away before the workday was over. What was he going to do? Fire her? She laughed to herself, finished her coffee, and left for work.

She had no trouble finding the tall glass skyscraper in downtown Atlanta. As she walked through the posh lobby and rode up the sparkling new elevator, she was very aware that Chad's company, Suncon, must have been doing very well to afford to locate their offices in such a building. But, on a moment's reflection, it didn't surprise her at all. Men like Chad always seemed to do well. Single-minded arrogance inevitably prevailed over common decency. Her mind went back to David. He was a very decent person, in spite of what he had done to her, but he could never succeed as Chad had obviously succeeded. And yet, Lauren would take someone like David a thousand times over anyone like Chad. David had always respected her judgment; he had seldom questioned her decisions. That was what she had always liked about him. She suddenly felt her loss very acutely. Just then she stepped off on the twenty-fourth floor.

To her left were large glass doors marked SUNCON, INC. She took a deep breath. This was really the beginning. She entered, a smile set firmly on her face.

"Good morning," she addressed the pretty young receptionist, a girl of about twenty, slim, with red hair and green eyes. That figures, she thought to herself. Chad Bently wouldn't surround himself with anyone but gorgeous young women who hadn't mastered the art of self-defense. This girl looked remarkably fresh—and remarkably naive. "I'm Lauren McCloud."

"Oh, good morning, Miss McCloud. I'm Jenny Wright." The girl extended her hand courteously.

"Nice to meet you," Lauren murmured.

"Mr. Bently told me to expect you. Come with me. I'll take you back to Mr. Patterson's office. He'll be showing you around today."

"Wonderful," Lauren remarked, following Jenny through the maze of desks. She couldn't have hoped for a better setup. But then, she should have realized someone else would have to show her around, because Chad had said he was hard at work, negotiating a contract. As they headed toward the executive offices, Jenny stopped any number of times to introduce Lauren to employees of all ranks. Just before they reached Mr. Patterson's office, the receptionist turned to Lauren.

"As soon as you have a bit of free time, let me know, Miss McCloud. Mr. Bently stressed to me what a kindness you were doing by helping out. And he put me in charge of introducing you to everyone in the office. I'd like to get that done, at your convenience, of course."

"Thank you very much, Jenny," Lauren responded, looking

back at the huge expanse of floor they had just covered. "If it's your job to introduce me to everyone, that's quite a job. This place is much bigger than I expected."

Jenny laughed. "If you think this is big, I hope you'll come back in a year. We're expanding again."

"Really?"

"Actually, the plans have been in motion a long time. We're just waiting for the company on the floor above us to move out. They leave in September. Then it will be really crazy. We've already all been given our assignments—which part of the move we're responsible for. Miss Ames, the former personnel director, helped Mr. Bently decide. Now that she's gone, we're going to have to get someone really good to replace her. Otherwise, this could easily be sheer chaos in six months."

Lauren laughed. "I'm amazed at how much you know about the inner workings of the company," she exclaimed cheerfully.

Jenny looked puzzled. "Everybody else knows as much as I do. We have weekly meetings. Mr. Bently conducts them himself. He tells us exactly what's happening in all aspects of the company."

Lauren shrugged. "That's very impressive," she said thoughtfully. "You have no idea how lucky you are to have such a conscientious boss. Most people don't."

"Well, this is kind of a special situation. We have a profit-sharing arrangement. We're all encouraged to take initiative. But listen"—Jenny glanced at her watch—"it's getting late. I'd better get you in to see Mr. Patterson. I'll tell you lots more about the company when you're through in there."

"I'd appreciate that."

Then they were standing in the doorway of an office marked GEORGE PATTERSON, VICE-PRESIDENT. Jenny entered first.

"Mr. Patterson? This is Miss McCloud."

The receptionist stepped aside. Lauren was facing a slender blond man, nervous and bespectacled. He smiled warmly as he rose to take Lauren's hand.

"Welcome to Suncon, Lauren. We're very pleased to have you on board, even if it is only for three weeks or so."

Jenny stood in the doorway. "I'll leave you two to get acquainted. See you later, Miss McCloud."

Lauren smiled at the receptionist, then focused her attention on George Patterson.

"It's great to be here," she responded cheerfully. "Everyone is exceptionally friendly."

George Patterson reached for the jacket hanging over his chair.

"Why don't we head out right now? I'm going to take you around the building sites. We can talk in the car."

Five minutes later she was sitting comfortably in an air-conditioned Buick. They pulled out of the underground parking lot.

"Yes," George was saying, "we really do have a nice crew here, enthusiastic and well educated. That's always been our criterion."

"Well, with a profit-sharing plan they all have a lot of motivation. I should think the personnel director's job is very easy. Hiring good people is easier when you have a lot to offer."

"The personnel director doesn't do the hiring," George remarked matter-of-factly, pulling up in front of a huge fenced-in excavation.

"The personnel director doesn't hire?" Lauren exclaimed, her eyes focused on the big Suncon sign beside the building site.

"No way." George looked her right in the eye. "Chad and I started out together. We both got our M.B.A.'s at Berkeley. And the basis of our theses was that management could not afford to isolate themselves from their employees. Constant interaction is all important. The most basic level of that is hiring. We've hired, that is, one of us has hired, every single employee who has ever worked for Suncon. Here, let's get out and take a look at our latest baby."

They walked toward a gate in the fence that surrounded the huge hole.

"But how can you possibly keep that up?" Lauren pressed him. "If you're planning on more expansion—realistically, you and Chad are only two people. You can't be everywhere all at once."

"Well, that *is* going to be a trick. But I guess it'll just mean we work longer and harder. I can't imagine either of us abandoning the principle that's been the basis of our success. And, quite frankly, I don't know anyone whose judgment we would trust as much as our own."

"I'm suitably impressed," Lauren remarked, as they advanced toward a small group of men, all wearing hard hats. One of the men turned in George's direction and waved. A minute later the whole group was gathered round Lauren and George.

"Hi, there, old man," a cocky young fellow addressed George.

The vice-president smiled. "Miss McCloud, I'd like you to meet Alfredo. He's the foreman on this site."

Lauren held out her hand, in a state of shock. This . . . *boy* was the foreman? It seemed incredible. His stained hand grasped hers.

"Howdy doody, Miss McCloud. It's sure a relief to see some other face than Uncle George's."

"It's a pleasure to meet you." Lauren smiled into Alfredo's dark eyes.

Alfredo put his hand over his mouth, as though he were telling a secret to the rest of the group.

"Hey," he said in a completely audible whisper, "shall we give our new personnel director a hard time, boys? What d'you say? Let's get out the union rules and drive her crazy."

Lauren smiled. "No fair . . . at least not until you've given me a chance to study. Then I'd be happy to have you give me a test. I should know the stuff inside out. And, if I don't, I'll have to keep studying until I do."

Alfredo stared at her quizzically. The other men were goading him on. Finally he addressed George.

"Hey, man, where did you get this one? She don't sound like Miss Ames at all. She's a real sport."

George glanced at Lauren. There was a smile sneaking across his face. "Listen, Alfredo, you know it's not your job to harass personnel directors. Why don't you stick to what you do best, which is introducing her to everyone?"

"Hey, Georgey, I like you." Alfredo laughed. "You tell it like it is. You come with me, Miss McCloud, and I promise you'll be safe. See ya later, Uncle George," he said cheerfully. But George followed anyway.

Alfredo led her around, introducing her to all the men on the ground. She got many appreciative looks and several out-and-out leers. She took all of it in stride, never losing her professional cool.

Later on, when they were back in the car, driving to the last building site—the last of four—Lauren's mind turned to Miss Ames, the former personnel director.

"George, Chad mentioned that Miss Ames had only given her notice Monday. Is she still around? I haven't seen her."

"No, she isn't. Circumstances dictated that she leave right away." Though his words were brief and to the point, Lauren read a world of meaning in them. She nodded.

"Oh, I see" was all she said.

There was a brief silence, then George laughed, a wry low laugh.

"No, I don't think you do see, Lauren," he remarked with gentle humor. "It wasn't that she was fired. She had a disagreement with us about company policy, that's all." He paused. "I don't want any mystery surrounding her. It was her decision to leave immediately—completely hers. She was one sharp lady, but . . . I guess everybody has their limitations."

"That goes without saying." Lauren glanced through the window at the hot city sidewalks. Somehow, the brief discussion had left her feeling uncomfortable. It shouldn't have, but it did. Why? She didn't really know. But she couldn't help wondering what had brought about the sudden parting of ways. After all, it could be something that would affect her own position. Then she dismissed the idea. It didn't matter. She would only be there three weeks—and she could easily imagine that Chad Bently would be an impossible person to work with for any longer than that.

They made their last stop, then returned to the office. Before riding up on the elevator, George took her to the cafeteria, where they bought sandwiches and fruit juice. They sat in her new office and ate them, amicably.

"I think you should spend the afternoon looking over these union booklets."

Lauren nodded, scrutinizing the stack of six directly in front of her.

George continued. "Don't laugh when I tell you these are the short versions. Believe me, if any workmen's-comp problems arise while you're here, we'll have to take out the big bound issues—they've got all the fine print."

"How well I remember." Lauren sighed. "When I interned at the plastics factory, I practically had the large manual memorized. But I can see very clearly we're working with a much more complex union situation."

"Don't sweat it. If anything gets too tricky, we just call up the lawyer. He takes care of all our really nasty problems."

"How nice!" Lauren exclaimed. "If I don't have to hire or deal with nasty problems, this job sounds wonderful."

"Well, you get to do the things you're trained to do. There's quite a bit of testing and analysis to be done. And, of course, there's a fair amount of counseling. Our big deal is productivity. People can't reach their highest potential unless they're doing what they should be doing at any given moment."

"Jenny Wright was saying you have pretty loose job definitions," Lauren remarked, much interested in what she was learning.

"Experience—that's purely and simply how I sum up our approach. We like to try new things, instead of sticking to dead routines. That isn't to say we don't make mistakes. But I will say our rate of success is high."

"One of the papers eventually incorporated in my dissertation was about the failures of specialization. I think I understand exactly what you mean." Lauren nodded vehemently. "A lot of businesses forget how important the larger picture is. Most of the research I did indicated that, if employees were able to perform or, at the very least, fully understand, each step in a process, their work was far superior and ultimately productivity went up."

"That's exactly what we've discovered," George concurred. "Exactly. They feel a much greater degree of respect for each other and their work."

Lauren took a sip of juice and smiled, satisfied. "Who knows, George? I may just get a paper out of this little stint with your company. The possibilities are fascinating."

"Just be sure you mention my name, okay?" George stood up and stretched. "I think I'd better get back to work. If you have any problems, you know where my office is."

"Two doors down on the right, right?"

"You've got it." George was just leaving, his form framed by the doorway.

"Oh, by the way." Lauren tried to sound as matter-of-fact as she could. "I take it Chad isn't in the office at all today?"

"No, I don't think so," George replied. "As far as I know, he's going to be in Decatur County all day. Why? Did you need to talk to him?"

"Oh, no. Not at all. Just curiosity, that's all."

When George was totally out of sight, Lauren sighed and sank back in her chair. What luck! And with a little more luck he'd be tied up like this most of the time she was working at Suncon. That would enormously simplify everything. He'd be so busy he'd most likely forget all about his promise to show her around. She didn't care. She could always come back to Atlanta another time—sometime when she was quite sure Chad wouldn't be there.

And, as it was, she had decided she liked George Patterson very much. He would definitely be easier to work with than Chad. And yet, in spite of herself, Lauren found herself thinking about Chad. Whatever else she might think of him, it was certainly much to his credit that he had such an intelligent partner. And it was obvious that George respected Chad enormously.

Lauren reflected on their progressive management techniques. That was one of the things that had impressed her most, because it related directly to her own experiences and experiments at the plastics factory. Chad didn't, or at least hadn't, struck her as the type to go in for innovative thinking but . . . but from what

George had said, Chad had worked on this concept since college. And it wasn't just an ideal with him. The profit sharing and the weekly meetings were solid indications of that. Grudgingly, Lauren had to admit that she respected him for these efforts. The thought dismayed her somehow. She turned to her work, in an effort to forget these new feelings.

The afternoon passed very quickly. Though she had fully intended to skip out a little early, when she finally looked at the clock it was ten after five. George had left at four thirty, to stop by one of the construction sites. She closed the last little booklet, shaking her head to bring herself back to reality. It was intense reading. She was glad to have it finished. On her way to the elevator she noticed that the main office was almost totally empty. Oh, well, she thought. She wasn't in any particular hurry. After all, Chad wasn't around. She didn't have to worry about avoiding him.

She strolled out of the building, toward the underground parking lot. It was a gorgeous evening. The heat of the day was dissipating, a cool breeze wafted about, carrying the luxurious scent of dogwood. Her mind drifted back to Connecticut, the summer before. The smell of dogwood hadn't, of course, filled the air. The scent of wildflowers had taken its place. She and David had gone on a picnic down by the stream. It was the day they first actually discussed marriage plans.

As she wandered into the dark confines of the parking lot, she could remember that day as clearly as if it had been . . . yesterday. She reached her car, romantic images still floating through her head—romantic images coupled with pangs of regret. It wasn't until she put the key in the lock that she realized the door wasn't locked. And the second she realized that, her eyes met Chad's. He was lying languorously across the front seat, smiling at her. Lauren's face froze.

"What do you think you're doing? How did you get into my car?" She couldn't even bother to control her fury.

"Now, why would you be so upset?" Chad reflected, after a moment of careful thought.

"Are you crazy?" Lauren protested. "I come to my car in a

dark, deserted parking lot to find . . . you just sitting there . . . as if you owned it."

Chad laughed. "Why should you be surprised? I think you should be pleased. At least you know you're safe with me. Look at my track record. . . ."

"Don't you dare say another word. Get out of my car this second."

"Oh, do you want to take my car?" He swung his legs around, moving toward the door where she was standing.

Lauren sighed, exasperated, and crossed her arms over her chest.

"I want to take my car and go straight home. That's what I want to do."

"But you can't," Chad protested. "I've promised to take you out to dinner, then show you around the town. That's the very least you owe yourself after a long hard day . . . to say nothing of what you owe me for providing you with such a stimulating environment in which to spend your days." He stepped gracefully out of the car, still smiling.

Lauren fixed him with her gaze. He was impossible. There was no doubt about it. And he was right. This was part of the deal—dinner and sightseeing. If she persisted in resisting his invitation, it would look as though she were afraid to spend time with him, as if she couldn't handle it. Well, she hadn't had to spend any time with him today. To that extent she'd been lucky. But she'd known when she took him up on the offer that sooner or later she would have to be around him. Why not tonight?

After all, his idea for the evening and hers didn't have to coincide. He no doubt expected her to fall head over heels in love with him, totally intoxicated by his mere proximity—just like every other woman in his life. She wanted simply to have a good time—a great time, since she really did want to look around the city—and then go home to bed. Alone. She had agreed to dinner and sightseeing—nothing more. A smile, cool and gracious, broke from her lips.

"You're absolutely right. It has been a long day—but certainly nothing that a leisurely dinner and some entertaining sights wouldn't help to soothe."

A faint look of surprise passed through his eyes. "I'm so glad you've come around to seeing things my way. I promise you, you won't be disappointed."

He offered her his arm. "There's no way I could be disappointed," she murmured with quiet assurance. She kept her eyes straight ahead, but she could feel the curious glance he was giving her. Yes, she thought triumphantly, there was more than one way to skin a cat—and this was definitely the better of the two alternatives.

But, as they walked toward the black Jaguar sedan, she had to admit to herself that the firm pressure of his arm on hers filled her with a subtle but all-pervasive excitement. She was relieved when he released her and opened the door.

The evening started out on an entirely unexpected note. After leaving the parking lot, Chad wound his way out of the central business district. They left the glass and the glitter of modern Atlanta behind, still sparkling in the late-afternoon sun. When they pulled up in front of a huge old red-brick mansion, Lauren couldn't contain her curiosity.

"Where are we?" she asked, smiling. "Is this a restaurant?"

Chad laughed, an easy, infectious laugh. "No. That'll be later. I hope you don't mind waiting to eat."

She shook her head. "Not at all."

"Since we only have the evenings and most museums close by seven or eight, I thought we'd take a look at a few of them first."

"Is this a museum?" She smiled quizzically.

Chad didn't answer. He just smiled back and hopped nimbly out of the car. When he opened the door for her, all he said was, "You'll see."

They walked up several steps. When they reached the top there was a black sign, trimmed in white, reading simply, THE TOY MUSEUM. Lauren laughed in disbelief.

"A toy museum?" she exclaimed incredulously. This certainly didn't seem like the suave Chad she knew. But, intrigued, she resisted the impulse to comment.

"This isn't just any toy museum," he said, taking her arm to guide her in. "It's like some kind of fantasy land."

Inside, each room had been converted to display toys pertaining to a particular theme. The doll room was absolutely spectacular, filled with porcelain-faced creations, many from Europe, dating all the way back to the eighteenth century. Lauren couldn't help herself. Her natural enthusiasm got the better of her. She had to pick some of them up. They were all freestanding, to encourage people to touch them—to examine the enormously intricate costumes. They were fabulous, done in the most elegant fabrics.

"Oh, Chad," she exclaimed enthusiastically, holding one particularly gorgeous one out to him. "Can you believe this? Apparently this doll was fashioned to look just like her little owner. The display card says she's even wearing a copy of her owner's favorite dress! It's incredible."

Chad laughed, showing every bit as much excitement as Lauren felt. After leaving the doll room, they walked back to one of the rooms displaying mechanical toys. There were quite a few children in this room, but it was very, very quiet—except for the small sounds of the toys working.

They stood watching the children lost in their own special dreamworld. Lauren turned to Chad, smiling almost wistfully.

"I can't believe this," she said softly. "It's like a permanent Christmas."

"I know," Chad concurred quietly. "An old man is responsible for all of it. His philosophy is that toys are to be played with. When they wear out, he fixes them or puts them to rest in his storeroom downstairs."

"Have you been here a lot?" she asked distractedly, staring at one toy that showed Santa going down a chimney with a sack of toys, then coming out without it.

"George and I bring his kids here a couple of times a year. They have a great time but the funny thing is, I think adults enjoy it just as much. It really helps unwind. It makes me forget all the pressures of the day-to-day world. Come on, let's go over here and try out a few."

They stayed, going from room to room until it closed at seven. They were still laughing and giggling when they finally left. Back in the car, Lauren sighed.

"Now where to?" she asked with obvious interest.

"How about the High Museum of Art? They have a great collection of Impressionist art—and a lovely bar."

"Sounds wonderful!"

Twenty minutes later they were back in the center of the city, at the huge, modern Memorial Arts Building. The sun was almost down now. There was a slight chill in the air. As they walked into the building, Chad very casually put his arm around Lauren's shoulders. It was such a natural gesture, she didn't even think to object. Once they were inside, he dropped his arm away just as easily.

The collection was beautiful. In its soft, sensitive, slightly blurred view of life, it offered the perfect complement to the Toy Museum. They wandered off on their own, each one occasionally going to get the other to share a particularly stunning picture. It was a quiet, meditative time. Lauren couldn't help feeling pleased that Chad had brought her here.

They retired to the bar, an elegant modern place, done in an Impressionist palette of azure blue, pale mauve, and corn yellow. The furniture was all very soft looking, with rounded edges. The lighting was very subdued.

They sipped their drinks, chatting cheerfully about the paintings and the toys. Close to nine o'clock Chad rose, offering her his arm.

"Now for dinner."

"I can hardly wait. I'm starving!"

"Then I've accomplished my goal," he said with a smile, again slipping his arm around her shoulders.

She laughed. "You mean the purpose of all this was to get me hungry?"

He nodded. "You bet. The restaurant we're going to is one of my favorites. I wanted to be sure you'd really appreciate the food. That's the only reason I dragged you all over." They both laughed, and Lauren was startled to realize how much she was enjoying Chad's company.

The restaurant was charming. From the outside it looked like little more than a cottage. It was called Tante Hélène's and it fully lived up to its promise. The atmosphere was intimate, the food was scrumptious—fine French cuisine. Lauren ordered *tournedos*, which would have been excellent on its own but which seemed doubly delicious with the exquisite Rothschild Saint-Emilion Chad had selected. For dessert they feasted on the most fabulous crêpe suzette Lauren had ever tasted. Then they completed the meal with a cup of café au lait.

"Well," Chad said with a laugh, somewhat surprised, as they left the restaurant. He had slipped his arm around her shoulders once again. "I had thought we might go to see the monument in Kennesaw Mountain Battlefield Park, but it's getting a little late for a working girl."

"Late?" she responded, also surprised. And suddenly his arm around her shoulders made her nervous. It just felt too comfortable.

They had reached the car. After opening the door, he turned and looked her fully in the eyes.

"It's almost eleven thirty," he said quietly.

She shook her head in disbelief. "You're kidding," she exclaimed before she had a chance to consider her words.

"I'm glad the time seemed to go by so quickly for you—you know what they say about time flying when you're having fun. . . ." His voice was low. A smile, slow and assured, played around the corners of his mouth. Lauren grew slightly more anxious. She shrugged nonchalantly.

"I did enjoy myself, Chad."

"I could tell you did . . . I was pleased to see it was so easy."

She stared at him, struggling within herself for the right thing to say.

"You planned the evening perfectly . . . I wouldn't have expected anything less from you. . . ." she finally responded, trying to make her tone both cool and gracious.

He laughed, taking one small step toward her that suddenly

seemed to cut the distance between them from friendly to intimate. His hand slid down her arm. There was nothing casual in his touch. It sent a cascade tingling through her body. Her senses suddenly seemed more powerful and more acute. She drew instinctively back, only to feel the pressure of the car door against her back. Then he stepped a little closer. His masculine scent pervaded the air. His broad strong chest tempted closeness. She started to feel weakened by the sensual power of his nearness. His lips were right next to hers. She could feel their breath meeting and mingling in the cool night air.

"Please, Chad," she whispered, her voice hoarse with emotion. "We've had a lovely evening . . . let's go home."

"It wasn't just that I planned the evening well. You know that, Lauren. We were very compatible tonight—once you let down your guard. You enjoyed my company every bit as much as I enjoyed yours."

"Of course I did, Chad," she insisted with what little determination she could muster. "What did you expect me to do? Be miserable all night? I had every intention of enjoying myself—and I did."

"Then why are you suddenly trying to deny what you feel?" A spark of anger lit up in his eyes. "A minute ago you were happy to be close to me. You liked the feel of my arm around your shoulders. Why are you denying that?"

"I'm not! We can be friends. . . ."

"We can't be just friends," he insisted, leaning closer. "We can't, because that's not how either of us feels."

"Speak for yourself! You don't know anything about my feelings. Take me home, now. That's where I want to go."

"I don't believe you!"

"I don't care what you think," she asserted, trying to push past him. But his strong arm was in the way and, without a second's hesitation, it swept around her, pulling her very close. He stared into her eyes with an intensity that startled her.

"Please, Chad," she protested, just before his lips pressed powerfully against hers.

They were more demanding than ever before—more demanding than any lips had ever been. And his need was so urgent. That in itself was exciting. She tried to deny her own strong need to return the kiss but he wouldn't let her. Nothing would discourage him. His hand slipped, slowly, with aching sensuality, from her waist to her breast. Her breath quickened, but she didn't have the strength to push it away.

And his touch hadn't changed at all. With the pleasure he brought now came all the tumultuous memories of that passionate encounter five years earlier. Masterfully, through the thin summer fabric, his fingers caressed the soft flesh. Her mind was ablaze with the magnificent torrent of sensations that seemed to flow over each other, each one more powerful than the last. From the fiery pitch of emotion a moan broke from her throat— a moan of yearning and wanting.

His tongue was quick to seize the opportunity. Swiftly and surely it swept around the moist confines, asserting its right to be there. She felt as if he were tasting her very being—and she, his. She was rapidly losing control of the situation. She felt almost incapable of stopping her instinctive responses—and desperate to succeed. His body pressed fully against hers, making her realize only too acutely that his passion was every bit as intense as hers.

Finally, she managed to pull her mouth away. Her whole body was burning, awakened by desire; her mind was whirling, able to focus on one thing and one thing only.

"Lauren," he whispered huskily, his hand still resting on her breast, "I think we should go home—now."

She shook her head frantically. "Chad, no. I don't want to. I didn't want any of this to happen. I don't want anything between us."

He drew away, the passionate fire in his eyes quickly supplanted by anger.

"What do you mean by that?" he snapped.

She stepped away from him, frightened by his voice.

"I mean just what I said, Chad. I can't understand your reaction. You've known all along what my feelings are. I told you yesterday morning . . ."

"When are you going to face reality?" he demanded. "There already is something between us—something you started five years ago. You thought it was just a game. It wasn't. Do you still fool yourself about that?"

"I was young, Chad—inexperienced. You knew that. Nothing much happened. And that was your decision, not mine. If something more had happened, believe me, I'd take full responsibility for it. Please just forget the past. I've changed a lot. . . ."

"Nothing you say could ever convince me that you've kissed another man the way you were just kissing me. Did David kiss you the way I kissed you? Tell me the truth!"

Lauren took several steps back. Her whole body tightened.

"It's none of your business," she snapped, a mixture of exasperation and anger filling her. "It's none of your business at all. I don't have to talk about my personal life with you."

Chad glared at her. "If he had, you would have been only too happy to admit it, and you know it. He didn't and he couldn't. You're lucky he's out of your life. It's just too bad you're determined not to let anyone else in."

"You don't know what you're talking about!" she yelled.

"I know exactly what I'm talking about. Come on. I'm taking you home."

CHAPTER FIVE

They drove home in complete silence. Lauren was relieved to see the house wrapped in darkness. Susan and Greg were either out or already in bed. Thank God, she thought. She couldn't face talking to anyone—not now. But instead of pulling into the driveway, Chad stopped in front, leaving the motor going.

Lauren sat there a second, confused. He said nothing. She glanced over at him.

"Aren't you coming in?" she asked quietly.

His eyes met hers. "What I choose to do now has nothing to do with you. You've made that much perfectly clear."

"Oh, really?" she exclaimed angrily. "Because I didn't follow your little plan and show the proper degree of appreciation for the lovely evening?"

Anger flared in Chad's dark eyes. "That has nothing to do with it! Absolutely nothing—and you know it."

"I'm not so sure I do! What about me? Where did my feelings and needs fit in?"

"You fit in just perfectly. You did all evening," he said in a low voice that betrayed the control he was having to exercise. "Don't blame me if you can't admit that!"

"There's nothing to admit. . . ." she began to protest.

Chad turned away. "I'm not going to argue with you. I brought you home. That's what you said you wanted. If I'd had any idea what was in store for me, I would have listened to you to begin with."

"That's right!" Lauren exclaimed, opening the door. "You should have!"

"I would have listened to you, instead of assuming you were a mature adult!" Chad continued, ignoring her interruption. "You didn't let me finish what I had to say!"

Lauren jumped out of the car, more furious than ever.

"If you think your judgment of a person is the only one that counts, then you'd better think again!" she said, slamming the door.

"Have a good night's sleep, Lauren," he called as the car started to move away.

Lauren felt like kicking at the fender, but she wouldn't give him the satisfaction of seeing her so upset. He'd already upset her more than he had any right to. It was ridiculous! How had she allowed him to get to her like that? She raced up the stairs from the sidewalk, fumbled for her keys, and burst into the house. Thank God she was home! It was infinitely better than having to fend him off. Infinitely better.

She turned on a few lights, just to make the house seem inhabited, then walked slowly upstairs. It was a good thing he hadn't decided to come in. That would have ruined the whole point of coming home. And if he had come in, for all she knew he would have followed her right up to the moonlit cupola, still determined to have his way.

At this very moment he was probably on his way over to one of his many girl friends—someone who found him irresistible, of course. He was lucky so many women were willing to settle for so little! But she wasn't. She refused simply to be used and discarded. That had happened once already. She had no intention of letting it happen again. Yes, to that extent, Chad had been right. She wasn't going to let just anyone into her life. She would be very, very cautious the next time. The pain David had caused her was still too fresh to be forgotten.

The air in the cupola was cool and fresh. She had left one of the windows open. The breeze made her break out in goose bumps, yet she sank down on the bed without closing the window. Somehow, just being there was clearing her mind. She could feel herself coming back to reality, out of the heated emotional nightmare. At first it was a good feeling, but then she became strangely nervous. Her mind inevitably went back to Chad. She couldn't stop herself from reviewing the events of the evening. She could hear his voice, first humorous, then passionate, then stern and angry. She could see his eyes. She could feel his lips and his body, feel the need and the want he had expressed so fully. These thoughts made her shudder. She didn't want to remember. Not at all. Because remembering him made her remember how much she actually had responded. Part of her had wanted him—wanted him very much. But that wasn't the important part, and somehow she couldn't explain that to him.

She rose anxiously from the bed and began undressing. He couldn't understand why she didn't trust him, why she couldn't be free spirited enough to just give herself completely to the feeling of the moment. He couldn't understand how, after David, she was terrified of having her heart broken yet again. He couldn't understand that she wasn't used to being pushed around emotionally. No man had ever made such absolute claims on her. He couldn't do that, she muttered to herself, slipping into her silky gown. He couldn't. Not after what he had done to her, five years ago. Not after all the trouble he had caused between her and Susan.

Then, for some crazy reason, tears sprang into her eyes. Angrily, she tried to fight them back. Why should she cry? Why now? She'd gotten what she wanted. He was leaving her alone—for tonight, anyway. So why was she upset? She didn't have to think about him, not for one more second. And she wouldn't. But the tears streamed down her cheeks, first slowly, then uncontrollably. And the harder she cried, the more difficult it was to wipe his image from her mind, to erase the echo of his angry words from her memory. She hadn't done anything! She hadn't! He was wrong. She hadn't led him on. He had brought it all on himself. The more she thought, the more upset she got. Finally, she rolled over, burying her head in the pillow. Luckily, emotional exhaustion took its toll quickly. She fell asleep, almost before she knew it.

When she came down in the morning, she was startled to see

Susan dressed, sitting in the living room, drinking coffee. The moment Susan looked up, Lauren could see by the agitation in her eyes that she knew something. What had happened last night, while she lay sleeping?

"Morning, Susan," she said, as casually as she could. "Are you going someplace early?"

Susan studied her sister's face, as though she couldn't quite believe what she was hearing. "Chad told me you'd need a ride downtown," she finally said, slowly.

Lauren felt her cheeks color. That's right! How had she forgotten? They had left her car in the parking lot.

"It's okay, Susan, really. I'll just take a cab. Let me grab a cup of coffee. I'm running a little late." Lauren quickly headed into the kitchen. A second later Susan joined her.

"No, I'll drive you, Lauren," she said quietly but firmly, pouring herself another cup of coffee.

Lauren thought of arguing with Susan, then decided it would do more harm than good. She could tell by Susan's tone that her sister had something planned for the drive. If Lauren didn't go along with her, she'd just have to hear the good news sooner—and right now what she needed was a cup of coffee to steel her.

She gulped it down, using the morning newspaper as a way to escape talking to Susan. When she'd finished one cup, she looked up.

"If it's okay with you, Susan, I think we should leave now."

"Fine," Susan remarked almost cheerily. And, for just a second, Lauren felt very confused.

"I hate to drag you out in rush hour," she said as they pulled onto a busy road.

Susan shrugged. "I wanted to drive you, Lauren. I needed to talk to you."

"Oh, what about?" Lauren tried to sound unconcerned.

There was a brief pause. Susan shifted a little uneasily in the driver's seat.

"I know something happened last night," she finally said. "We were still up when Chad got home . . . well, it was obvious you weren't with him. It was also obvious he'd had more to drink than he usually does."

Lauren's cheeks burned. "Did he say anything?" she asked, having difficulty hiding her anxiety.

Another pause, brief but agonizing.

"No, no, he didn't say anything. Chad's not like that. He keeps things to himself."

"I just got tired after my first day of work. That's all, Susan. He brought me home early."

They drove a few blocks in silence.

"Lauren, I don't know exactly what happened, but naturally I'm a little worried. This whole idea of you working for Chad . . . it's just wrong, believe me. I think you should get out of it somehow. . . ."

"I'm not sure I can," Lauren protested. "I agreed to do it."

"If Chad's making your life difficult in any way, Lauren, that's the perfect excuse. You look so pale this morning. I know he upset you. Tell him right now, this morning, as soon as you go in, that you've changed your mind. Believe me, Lauren, it's for the best. I know Chad. I know him all too well. It's like I said. You simply can't trust a word he says."

"I know that," Lauren responded very quietly, feeling increasingly uneasy. Why was Susan pushing her like this? She liked to think Susan had her best interests at heart, but how could she speak so definitively unless she knew . . . unless Chad had told her something about last night? Could he have? Would Susan lie to her? Maybe she would, to save her younger sister the humiliation of knowing that someone else knew. That could be it.

But even if Susan did know, even if she did have Lauren's best interests at heart, she really couldn't address the subject of Lauren's professional life. Susan should know that Lauren couldn't just commit herself, then back out if it suited her purposes. She owed it to herself to make the most of this opportunity.

They pulled up in front of the building that housed Suncon. Lauren started to open the door. Susan reached out and touched her hand.

"I'm only trying to help, Lauren. That's all. I've seen him hurt so many women."

Lauren forced a reassuring smile onto her tense face. "Don't worry, Susan. Nothing happened—and nothing will."

Susan threw her hands up in the air. "Well, don't let me interfere. It's your vacation. If you want to sacrifice it to Chad Bently, go right ahead. Just don't come crying to me when you get burned. I've warned you."

"I know, Susan—and I do appreciate your concern. Believe me. Listen, let's just forget about Chad. We don't have to think about him unless he's around. Come down and meet me for lunch someday."

Susan's anxious expression gave way to a smile. She nodded. "Sounds great. I'll find a good day."

"Oh, and Susan," Lauren remarked thoughtfully, "remind me to get you to sign those legal papers for Dad. With all of this going on, I'm liable to forget. He'd be so upset if I did."

"Sure," Susan said, turning away. "Well, you'd better get in there and I'd better get going. Talk to you later."

Lauren watched Susan's car pull into the heavy traffic. Only a minute later it had disappeared in the maze. She took a deep breath and headed into the building. She sincerely hoped Chad wasn't in the office. Now that she suspected he had spoken to Susan about her, probably in a drunken fit, her anger flared again. How dare he come between Susan and herself, simply for his own selfish reasons! What had he told Susan, to make her this upset?

And then, suddenly, something occurred to her. Susan had been really pushing her to leave the job. Lauren couldn't understand it unless . . . unless Chad was the one who had suggested it. That made sense. Having made such a big deal about asking Lauren to help, he was no doubt too embarrassed to ask her to leave so suddenly—now that it was clear he wasn't going to get what he was after. Susan was probably very upset, being torn between Lauren and Chad. No wonder she was so agitated. It was unforgivable of Chad to involve Susan in that way—and he wasn't going to get off easily.

Now that she had figured out his game plan, Lauren decided nothing would make her leave Suncon until the three weeks were up. She would force him to deal with her professionally, as regularly and as often as she could manage it. And just before she left, she would have the pleasure of telling him off. It would be a small revenge, but a just one.

And this realization made her feel much better about Susan. Because, otherwise, she'd have to imagine that Susan was trying to keep her away from Chad, for some reason known only to herself. And that might mean . . . But it didn't matter what it might mean. It wasn't possible that Susan would be trying to keep her away from Chad. The other explanation was far more plausible.

As she pushed the door open, Jenny Wright was just returning to the receptionist's desk.

"Miss McCloud, I'm glad you're here. Mr. Bently wants to see you the minute you arrive."

"Oh," Lauren exclaimed, a little startled, "I didn't realize he was in the office today."

Jenny laughed. "Neither did I. Maybe *you'll* find out why he came in. It must have been something important, because I had to cancel two meetings for him."

"I'm sure I will find out," Lauren remarked quietly, taking firm strides in the direction of her office. But after she had gone about ten feet she stopped, turning back to Jenny. "I don't know where Mr. Bently's office is." She smiled to hide her embarrassment.

"Oh, no problem," Jenny reassured her. "It's just past George Patterson's, at the end of the hall. The door is open."

Lauren nodded, then continued on her way. She didn't have any idea what he had in mind, but it really didn't matter. She was firm in her resolve. The only thing that still wasn't clear in her mind was exactly what she would say to him. But his behavior would quickly settle that issue.

She set her purse down and, grabbing a paper and pen, headed down the corridor. She would begin by acting as if this were simply and exclusively business. That was definitely the best way to start.

When she reached the doorway, he was standing with his back to her, his shirt-sleeves rolled up, looking out the window and dictating a letter to a young secretary. Normally Lauren would have walked away, not wanting to interfere. But he had said he wanted to see her immediately upon her arrival, so she waited. A second later the secretary glanced up and smiled.

"Mr. Bently, Miss McCloud is here." She rose and headed for the door, without his having to say a word. He turned slowly around. When the secretary had slipped out, he spoke.

"Why don't you close the door and sit down?" he said very quietly. She followed his instructions, all the while thinking how tired he looked. It was his own fault for drinking so much—and for staying up late to talk to Susan.

They stared at each other for at least a minute. Lauren's gaze didn't flinch once. He had asked to see her, he would speak first. And finally he did.

"I owe you an apology for my behavior last night," he began, his voice low and determined. Lauren nodded slightly, not knowing what else to do. She hadn't expected him to say anything of the sort, not after the way he had spoken last night. After a respectful pause, indicating she had the option to speak, he went on.

"Unfortunately, I can't say it won't happen again." A faint smile, a very attractive smile, played on his lips for a second. Lauren tensed. She was totally confused.

"I'm not sure I understand what you're getting at," she remarked.

"What I'm getting at is, quite bluntly, that I don't think I should take you around sightseeing—it wouldn't be fair, for all sorts of reasons. Since this is your vacation and you haven't been to Atlanta before, I don't think it's appropriate for me to deprive you of the opportunity. And if I can't keep my half of the deal, I don't think you should be forced to keep yours."

Now she understood. She rose, controlling her anger. So he was waging an out-and-out campaign to get rid of her. Or perhaps he had called Susan and discovered her older sister had failed on her assigned mission. This whole meek performance, complete with the handsome, shy smile, was nothing more than a game, a ploy to make her agree to go.

"No," she said with all the calm of confidence. "I'd like to stay and do the job I agreed to do. I took it on as a professional enterprise. I'm still capable of seeing it that way."

A look of total confusion and surprise spread across Chad's face. Lauren didn't allow her own satisfied smile to surface. It was enough to see that he knew she had caught him at his game.

"But what about the sightseeing?" he finally said, very slowly, with obvious surprise.

Lauren shrugged nonchalantly. "I'll just have to make another trip to Atlanta. I certainly don't intend to lose a moment's sleep over it."

For just a split second Lauren thought he sighed with relief. And she saw a familiar sparkle in his eyes. But that vanished, replaced almost instantaneously by a serious professional expression.

"Well, since that's settled, let's get to work. I ran an ad in Monday's paper. We've already had several applications. Why don't you take them back to your office?" He handed her a file folder. "I've already looked them over. I think we should interview every single one of them. I won't be around much, so I'll leave it to you to set up the interviews. But make sure to coordinate them with George's schedule. I'd definitely like him to be in on it. Once you've narrowed down the field, I should have a little more free time. Then we'll all get together."

Lauren nodded and headed toward the door. She had her hand on the knob, when she suddenly decided to turn back.

"Oh, by the way, I want you to know I appreciate the apology," she said, smiling. "Jenny mentioned you had to cancel a couple of meetings to be here. I hope you're pleased with the results of your efforts." There was just a hint of sarcasm in her voice. Chad smiled back, visibly confused.

"Of course I am," he finally said. "I think I did much better than I'd hoped to."

Lauren stared at him. His tone sounded very sincere, and yet she knew he couldn't be. It was just a show. He probably was simply pleased to have the opportunity to continue bothering her. But he would be sorely disappointed. Very sorely disappointed.

"I'm glad you feel that way," she remarked. "It's amazing how far good manners will get you."

A hurt look flashed across his face. She had hit home. She fully expected him to give her some smart-alecky reply—but he said nothing. A second later she was out the door, grateful to have left him behind.

Back in her office, she glanced over the resumés. There had been eleven in only two days. At this rate they'd be swamped by the end of the week. With luck she'd be so busy she wouldn't be able to think about anything else. Maybe that was his idea of punishment for staying on the job. But he'd have a rude awakening, once he realized she loved her work, absolutely loved it.

The rest of the morning passed busily but uneventfully. Luckily, George Patterson was at his desk shortly after Lauren returned to her office. She was able to discuss the scheduling of interviews, then spend the rest of the morning setting them up. At five to twelve George was standing in the doorway of her office.

"Why don't I act like a civilized person and take you out for a bite to eat?"

Lauren smiled gratefully, grabbing her shoulder bag from the back of her chair.

"I won't pretend I'm not interested in anything as mundane as food. I'm absolutely starved."

It wasn't until they were walking out of the office that she realized she hadn't felt the least bit interested in food, first thing this morning. But the interview with Chad had resolved a lot of her tensions. It looked very much as though her life was going to be normal again.

"So," George began as they walked out into the hot sun, "did you see Chad this morning?"

Lauren started ever so slightly.

"Yes, ah, yes," she replied, collecting her thoughts. "I guess he left shortly after that."

"He canceled two meetings to see you. What did he want to talk to you about?"

There was something in his voice that bothered Lauren. He was open and yet . . . and yet, she couldn't put her finger on it. Maybe he just sounded more interested than usual.

"Oh, I guess he must just feel very protective. He wanted to discuss the hiring we had to do, that's all."

"Really?" George sounded clearly surprised. They had entered another skyscraper and were ascending on an elevator. "I'll tell you something, Lauren. I've known Chad for half his life—eighteen long years. We've worked together for twelve of those years. I've never known him to cancel a meeting for anything or anyone before. I had hoped he had to discuss something a little more important than hiring a personnel manager. You're sure you don't have any juicy office gossip for me?" He smiled broadly at her. She couldn't help smiling back, though she was distinctly uncomfortable.

"I'm afraid not," she replied. "Though I must say I should be flattered by the fact that he made such an enormous exception for me—I am flattered."

They were seated in a wide-open restaurant, surrounded by windows providing a panoramic view of the city. Lauren couldn't help but admire it.

"This place always impresses people from out of town," George kidded her. "Even jaded New Yorkers."

Lauren laughed. "Well, I'm glad you're treating me like a tourist. I don't imagine I'll have much opportunity to look around—this way I can do it all at once."

"Oh, really," George remarked thoughtfully. A waiter handed them menus, but George took Lauren's away. "Let me order for you. I know their specialties." Before the waiter had had a chance to get away, George muttered something to him about steak, then turned his attention back to Lauren. "Correct me if

95

I'm wrong, but Chad mentioned something to me about showing you around in the evenings. I thought that was part of the deal."

Color rushed to Lauren's cheeks. "Well, I guess he's busy . . . and after all, I did come down here to see my sister. We want to spend as much time together as possible—she'll be showing me around some."

George sat back. He was looking down at the table and shaking his head ever so slightly. His expression was amused.

"I think I'm going to have to have a chat with my buddy," he said reflectively. "He's used this company long enough as an excuse to avoid the attentions of beautiful women."

"Oh, I really don't think you need to speak to him on my behalf, George. Really. Chad and I understand each other perfectly."

"I wouldn't be speaking to him necessarily on your behalf, Lauren. I just think he works too hard. Anyone who can't take time off to show a pretty woman around—why, I'd show you around if I weren't happily married. Marriage is what helps me keep my sanity, in this crazy business world. I can leave it all behind when I go home. Forget it even exists. I've never been able to understand how Chad can't see that. He never makes any excuses for himself; never gives himself the time off any normal person needs. He's always got to be there, doing everything."

Lauren smiled, plentifully amused. "I don't believe a word you're saying, George. You're as hard working and as intelligent as any man I've ever met. I think Chad probably just likes to play the field—all his girl friends. My God, he's probably famous for running around. No wonder he's so busy. I don't think it's work at all!"

George laughed a confused but amiable laugh. "Wait a second. Slow down. It sounds to me like you've got several facts wrong."

"I hope you're not going to deny that he has a lot of girl friends. There are so many beautiful girls working in the office, he shouldn't even have to look elsewhere."

"Chad has never had anything to do with any woman in the office, Lauren," George said leaning toward her. "Let's begin by getting that straight. It's a matter of principle with him. And since I trust you, I'll also say that's the reason we parted ways with Miss Ames."

"Really?" Lauren exclaimed, unable to disguise the shock this revelation had caused her.

George leaned back, shrugging. "I fool you not. Chad Bently is a man of his principles. I must say sometimes I've disagreed with him—maybe I even disagreed with him about Miss Ames. She was beautiful *and* intelligent. But it's up to him. This company is everything to him, and he's worked harder than any man to make it better than I would have imagined possible."

"Why are you so humble, George? You started it with him. Take a little credit for yourself."

"I take a little credit and a big paycheck, that's all, Lauren. No, I don't think you understand. Chad and I started out together, but he's the brains. Definitely. And he's the progressive thinker. I understand his ideas. I help him implement them. I'm good with people—most of the time. But he's the instigator and always has been. Wait. Just watch him these next few weeks. It's hard for anyone who hasn't seen him close up to understand his particular fanatical form of dedication. He's the most determined person I've ever met. If he gives someone his word, they don't need a contract. I've never known him to let anyone down."

"You make him sound perfect—like superman," Lauren remarked disbelievingly.

"In some ways he is," George pronounced, as steak platters were set in front of them.

"This looks fantastic, George," Lauren exclaimed, glad for the opportunity to change the subject.

"You don't get to return to the office until you've finished every last delicious bite. How's that for discipline?"

"Your kids must love you—I assume you have kids?" she replied.

George raised his eyebrows jokingly. "Let's save that for another lunch. Our fourth is on the way."

"Four!" Lauren exclaimed. "Don't you believe in zero population growth?"

"To tell you the truth," George began, after finishing a huge bite, "I've never much thought about it. That's what happens when you grow up in California. You get used to seeing a lot of people."

"That's no excuse at all," Lauren continued playfully.

George gulped down some ice water. "You're right. I'm stretching the truth. Actually, the real reason we have four is that we just happen to like kids. It's no big deal. They're just habit forming." He laughed. "That's what Chad needs. A couple of kids. I really have the feeling it would change his life."

"I don't think so, George. Not if he's a workaholic. Children would just complicate matters." Lauren spoke seriously and thoughtfully.

"No, no. I didn't say he was a workaholic," George protested. "He knows how to relax. He just doesn't choose the methods I happen to approve of. He's an avid squash player. That's fine. He also swims—almost made the Olympic team, when he was in college. And he loves to travel. He goes to all sorts of exotic places."

"It sounds to me as though his life is complete." Lauren shrugged.

George demolished the better part of his steak before speaking again. He seemed lost in his own thoughts. Lauren didn't interfere. She was busy eating, too, and she was also hopeful the subject might change. No such luck. Over coffee the discussion continued.

"Lauren, Chad's life *is* complete in many ways. I don't think that's the issue. I just sometimes get the feeling he'd be happier if he found someone compatible to share it with. . . ." George laughed. "Look at us, trying to figure out Chad's life. He's probably the last person in the world who needs someone else to take care of him." Then he hesitated. "The funny thing is," he continued, in a more thoughtful vein, "that I don't think I've ever talked about Chad to another human being other than Ellen, my wife."

Lauren stared straight ahead. "He must have been very much on your mind today," she said, trying to sound casual.

George shook his head. "No, that's not it. I think the truth of the matter is that I like you and I trust you. I don't mean to flatter you, but there aren't a lot of people I trust." George rose, offering her his arm, and they left the restaurant in companionable silence.

Back at the office, George walked her down the corridor leading to their respective cubbyholes—small, but very comfortable. "Hey, I've got a great idea," he said suddenly. "Maybe Ellen and I will have you and Chad to dinner some night. I think that would be fun. How about it?"

"Oh," Lauren said, startled. "Of course, that sounds just wonderful."

"Great! I'll call Ellen this afternoon and suggest it."

Lauren was relieved when he finally left. She closed her eyes, seriously resisting the need to scream. What was going on? Was this some kind of grand conspiracy? Oh, God, she thought, sinking into her chair. This was the last thing she needed. George didn't seem like the type to play matchmaker, but he seemed unusually determined to tell her all about marvelous, illustrious Chad Bently.

Spare me, she thought. George was absolutely the most naive person she had ever met—and his naiveté threatened to make her life very difficult. Didn't he see what a self-serving, duplicitous character his friend was? Blind friendship, that was the only explanation. The trouble was, George was so good hearted she'd feel like a jerk not accepting his invitation. His good-heartedness probably prevented him from seeing the truth about Chad.

Well, before this disastrous evening ever took place, she had every intention of making it perfectly clear to Chad that none of this was her idea—none of it. And, if he so much as laid one finger on her . . . He wouldn't have the nerve to. She could tell she had finally intimidated him, this morning. He would certainly leave her alone.

This realization calmed her down; in no time at all she was back at work, preparing for the first interview, scheduled for three P.M. To avoid talking to George about anything but business, she didn't call him to her office until the candidate arrived.

Bruce Averol was thirty-one. According to his resumé he had just moved to Atlanta from Detroit, where he had worked for one of the major auto companies. On paper his credentials were striking. He had his doctorate in organizational psychology from Stanford; he had earned his M.B.A. from Princeton. He had five years of work experience. But the minute he walked in, Lauren had misgivings.

She didn't judge people by appearances, but she couldn't help noticing his stiff, uncompromising manner. Everything about him seemed to indicate a rigidity she was sure would not work in the Suncon context. George seemed to pick up on that also. Lauren was very impressed at the easy but pointed way George got Bruce Averol to reveal his particular biases.

To Mr. Averol's credit he didn't try to change his views to match theirs, once it became apparent the differences were significant. When he left, an hour later, George slouched down in the chair.

"One down and ten to go," he said, smiling.

"I'm suitably impressed," Lauren remarked. "I can understand why you like to be in on the hiring. You have a way with people."

George pulled himself up and rose. "Years of experience as a front man, Lauren. But wait till you see Chad at work. He's the toughy. He figures anyone who can survive an interview with him is his kind of person."

Lauren stifled a smile. "I'm just glad I didn't have to go through the interview."

"You must have," George responded. "In one way or another you must have. He's sneaky about stuff like that—and ultimately I'd have to admit he's a better judge of people than I am. It's almost eerie, sometimes, the way he can predict their behavior—and he won't even have known them that long, either."

"Oh, really," Lauren remarked with considerable interest.

"I kid you not. You're bound to see an instance of it, sometime or other. Just tell me if you're not impressed."

"I'm sure I will be," Lauren murmured quietly.

"Well, I guess it's back to the salt mines. I have a few more papers to read and sign, before I call it a day."

"We're going to be spending the whole day together, tomorrow," Lauren remarked, glancing at a paper in front of her. "Six interviews. If each one takes an hour . . ."

"Forget that." George laughed. "I was just indulging this fellow, today, mostly for your benefit. Chad and I have a signal. When either of us feels like we've seen enough to make a judgment, we wink twice. Then we both stand up and walk to the door."

Lauren couldn't help laughing. "Talk about tact!" she exclaimed. "I can't believe you guys, I really can't."

"Welcome to the real world, Lauren. Our time is very valuable. No one who's ever ended up working for us has elicited that response. We're infallible."

"Are you sure you're not giving a dangerous weapon to a stranger, by telling me this?" Lauren was still laughing.

"No . . . not at all. It's like I said, I trust you. Oh, and by the way, I haven't been able to reach Ellen yet. I'm not sure what she's up to."

"Well, there's certainly no hurry." Lauren hid her relief.

"We'll do it soon, anyway. I'll probably be able to tell you a date tomorrow."

He smiled and left. The last hour of the afternoon passed quickly. But Lauren knew she didn't have to worry about the time she left. She was sure Chad wouldn't be waiting in her car—she was sure and she was also relieved. She anticipated a very quiet evening alone with Susan and Greg. And it was a lovely thought.

101

CHAPTER SIX

When Lauren pulled up in front of the house, Greg was just getting out of his car. He hurried over and opened the door for her.

"Hey, there, I missed you last night," he exclaimed, smiling cheerfully.

"The feeling is entirely mutual," Lauren said, as they climbed the stairs.

Greg's face clouded. "Didn't you have a good time with Chad? I thought he was taking you out to dinner?"

"Oh, yes, of course we had a good time. It's just that it would have been so much nicer if you and Susan had come along."

They were in the house now. Greg's attention was immediately captured by a note in Susan's handwriting. It was addressed to him and placed prominently on a small table beside the door. Lauren was relieved by the obvious interest he took in it. For what seemed to be about the fiftieth time that day, the conversation was not going in the direction she wanted it to. She walked past him, dropping her bag and some papers on a chair in the living room.

"What time does Susan get home?" she called casually. "I thought we could rustle up dinner together—something suitably gourmet."

Her inquiry was met by a prolonged silence. So prolonged, in fact, that Lauren retraced her steps from the kitchen. Greg was still standing in the hall, staring at the note. His expression was very serious—and very sad.

"Greg?" Lauren spoke hesitantly. "Is something the matter?"

He stared at the paper for a second longer. Then he looked up and laughed halfheartedly.

"No, everything's okay." But he sounded somewhat less than convinced.

"Where's Susan?" Lauren pressed him, growing more concerned.

Greg shrugged. "I guess she's gone out to dinner with some friends. That's what the note says."

Lauren laughed, a confused laugh. "That's curious, Greg. Does she do this often? I mean, she must have known you were coming home . . . couldn't she have called you at the office?"

He led the way into the living room, silently. He stopped by the bar.

"You just don't know your sister, Lauren. She wouldn't call. It's not like her. When she wants to do something, she just does it. She doesn't risk having me say no. Come on. You and I are perfectly capable of having a lovely evening together. I'll even help you make dinner. That's something Susan won't let me do, when she's ruling the kitchen."

"Sounds great." Lauren forced herself to sound enthusiastic.

"Do you want a drink?" Greg pulled out a bottle of Scotch.

"Why not? How about another one of those delicious gin and tonics?"

"You've got it. So, what'll we make for dinner? I think we have a lot of cubed beef for shish kebab. How does that sound?"

"Couldn't be better—as long as you chop the onions."

"It's a deal." Greg disappeared into the kitchen for just a second, returning with a bucket of ice. He filled Lauren's tall glass with ice. "Hey, where's Chad? If you're not going out tonight, he should be coming home, too."

"Oh." Lauren started. Hadn't they gotten off the subject? Why did the conversation always have to come back to Chad? "I think he mentioned something about a business engagement. I think he'll be pretty late."

Greg shook his head in dismay. "I always thought I was a hard worker, but Chad's really too much." He handed Lauren her drink. "Well, since we'll only have each other tonight, why don't we toast my going away? It seems no one else is particularly interested."

"You're going away?" she exclaimed.

He smiled nonchalantly. "Tomorrow morning at six A.M. Your local world traveler boards a plane for yet another exotic location. This time my destination is somewhere in the mountains of Mexico."

She sank down on the couch, making no effort to hide her astonishment.

"But, Greg, how long will you be gone?"

He sat down across from her. "Oh, I don't know. Probably two weeks, minimally. If all goes well, I'll be back in time to wish you a cheerful farewell. If not . . . well, I'll just have to send a telegram."

Lauren sat there, trying to control her agitation. She shouldn't ask him—and yet she had to.

"Does . . . does Susan know?" she finally blurted out. "Does she know you're going away?"

Greg laughed, not a happy laugh. It was more philosophical amusement. Then he took another large gulp of his Scotch.

"That's probably the reason she decided to go out tonight."

Lauren shook her head, confused. "I don't get it. What are you saying?"

Greg leaned forward, then sank back again. He rubbed his forehead.

"Hey, listen, Lauren. You sister is your sister. You should be free to deal with her on that basis. Not with all this other garbage I've been loading on you."

Lauren was quiet for a moment, carefully considering her next words. "I appreciate what you're saying, Greg. I really do. But I don't think you understand how I see the problem." She stopped, as Greg downed the rest of his glass and rose to go to the bar. He returned with another glass of Scotch—but this time he had just skipped the ice completely. Lauren fought the urge to stop him and continued. "I'm just as concerned about Susan as you are. I can sense she has problems—at least, she doesn't seem very happy. . . ."

Greg's laugh was getting more uncontrolled. "That's because I try too hard to please her. . . . That's the problem. . . ."

"No, I don't think so, Greg." Lauren hesitated. "Surely you know Susan and I haven't been the best of friends over the years. Well, seeing Susan here, now, I can tell she's still very much the way she used to be. I don't think it's you, Greg. I think it's something about her personality. It's almost as if she's determined that no one will make her happy. . . ."

Greg was almost finished with his second glass of Scotch. He was slouched down so far that Lauren had trouble hearing him.

"What did you say?" she urged, after a lengthy, indecipherable murmuring.

He pulled himself up. Lauren was relieved—he didn't look as drunk as she had thought he was. But her relief was short lived.

"Let me get another drink, then I'll try to remember what I said." He got up and managed to walk fairly soberly to the bar and back. No ice cubes again. The glass was so full it was spilling. He propped himself up at the end of the couch.

"Lessee now," he said, taking a long drink. "Oh, yeah, I was saying something about Susan being right." He stopped, a serious expression on his face. The silence lasted three or four minutes. Finally, Lauren prompted him.

"Right about what?"

"Right about marrying me . . . I mean about who she should have married. . . . She shouldn't have married me. . . . She should have married . . . married . . . who should she have married? . . . I had it just a second ago."

"I don't know," Lauren replied, leaning forward with real concern. "Who should she have married?"

"Oh, yeah," Greg exclaimed triumphantly. He took another drink. "She should have married Chad. . . . That's who she said she wanted to marry. . . ."

"Chad," Lauren repeated almost to herself, a mixture of surprise and dismay in her voice.

". . . instead of an affair," Greg mumbled on. "It's just the idea of what she's doing . . . I should just leave, but I can't. . . ." He started crying, his head bent over the third empty glass of

Scotch. Lauren rushed over to him and put her arms around his quivering shoulders.

"Greg," she said, when the sobs had stopped for a moment, "is Susan having an affair with Chad?"

Greg started to laugh, a strange noise to come so quickly after body-wrenching sobs. He moved away from Lauren, heading toward the bar again. She glanced at her watch. He'd already had eight or ten ounces of Scotch, maybe more, and they'd been talking only half an hour. She felt scared. She followed him, taking hold of his arm as he started to pour.

"Haven't you had enough, Greg? I don't want you to get sick," she pleaded with him.

He turned his sad face toward her. "Please, Lauren. Tonight . . . I just have to, tonight." He filled the tumbler. She dropped her hand. Who was she to say it was wrong, when someone was hurting as badly as he was? She guided him back to the couch. He sat down, staring into his glass.

"No . . . no, you don't understand," he said desperately.

"What don't I understand?" Lauren asked.

"No . . . no, she's not having an affair with Chad. I didn't mean that at all . . . not at all. He's my brother. He wouldn't do that. No, I trust him completely, I really do . . . no, no, I'm wrong. She's not having an affair at all. It's just my imagination." He looked up at Lauren and tears sprang to his eyes again. "I shouldn't have told you any of this . . . none of it's true. Please believe me, Lauren. Please. Don't think badly of Susan. I imagine all these things. None of it has ever happened. I know it. I'm just drunk."

Lauren rubbed his back consolingly. "There, there," she said quietly, "don't worry about anything. I think I'd better get you something to eat."

Greg leaned heavily against her. The empty glass dropped from his hand.

"Please don't . . . please don't say a word to Susan about this. It'll just make her angry to know I'm still suspicious . . . I just can't help it . . . I have to be more understanding. . . ."

Lauren glanced at the kitchen. There was no way she was

going to get him to eat dinner—he could barely sit up. She had to get him to bed before he passed out on the couch.

"Don't worry, Greg. I promise I won't say a word. Now, listen, I'm going to get you upstairs—come on, let me help you up."

She took hold of his hands, pulling with all her might. His body was totally limp; it was no mean task. But finally he was sitting up. He seemed totally incoherent, but he did nod when she asked if he could make it upstairs. They started toward the stairs. They had gone only a few feet when he began to fall, knocking over a table and dragging her with him. At that very second Lauren heard the front door open and close. All she could think was, dear God, please don't let it be Susan.

"What's going on?" Chad's voice rang in her ears. She couldn't look up, but she'd never been so relieved to hear his voice. Suddenly she felt Greg's weight lifted off her. A second later she was helped to her feet by a strong swift pull. Chad's face was full of shock and real concern. "Lauren, what happened?"

"Greg drank too much. It's a long story . . . we've got to get him upstairs."

"I'll carry him to his bed." In an easy motion Chad picked his brother up and started up the stairs.

Lauren rushed into the kitchen, grabbing the first pot she found. As she hurried after Chad, she noticed the hall clock. It was only eight thirty. She hadn't expected Chad to come home so early, but thank God he had, thank God, she muttered to herself.

She and Chad spent the next hour by Greg's side, trying to ease his discomfort. Unfortunately, cool towels and Gatorade had very limited effect. He was sick so much they barely had time to look at each other, let alone speak except for the information they absolutely had to exchange.

Finally, Greg dozed off. They stayed quietly, one on each side of his bed, for about ten minutes, until Chad looked at Lauren and nodded. Together they left the room. They were just walking down the stairs, when Susan entered the house. She glanced up at them, very surprised.

"Where are you two coming from—or should I ask?" She smiled a little weakly.

Lauren was still so caught up in the events of the last couple of hours, she couldn't even begin to register the meaning of Susan's comment. She just stared at her sister, totally dumbfounded. She almost didn't notice Chad taking her elbow, leading her the rest of the way down.

"Well," Susan continued, looking increasingly uncomfortable, "I think I'll sit outside for a while. It's a beautiful evening."

"You might want to go up and take a look at your husband first."

Chad's words caught Susan totally by surprise. She stopped in midstep, turning to him with a shocked expression.

"What?" she said with real concern. "Has something happened to Greg? You should have told me right away."

"He got very drunk," Chad finally said.

The surprise faded from Susan's eyes. She laughed incredulously.

"He got drunk? Greg? You've got to be kidding. I never thought I'd live to see the day. But it's not the end of the world. Everyone has a fling from time to time. His is long overdue."

"It wasn't just a little fling, Susan," Chad interrupted. "He's been sick to his stomach for the last hour."

Her eyes seemed locked into Chad's. And, again, Lauren sensed a world of meaning passing silently between them. Finally, Susan spoke.

"Well, that happens sometimes, too. I just wish he'd been more careful. I'm sorry the two of you had to take care of him." It was a sincere apology but there was more—much more in her voice. She sounded both hurt and confused. Lauren wanted to ease the pain her sister was obviously feeling, but she wasn't sure what to do or say. There was something going on between Chad and Susan, and Lauren felt out of her depth.

"Lauren was here with him through most of it." Chad's voice broke the silence. "I didn't get home until an hour ago. It was a good thing I got home then. He'd collapsed on Lauren, in the hall. She was trying to get him to bed."

Susan's intent gaze shifted from Chad to Lauren. She laughed from embarrassment.

"Thanks, sis," she said quietly. "I hope he wasn't too much trouble."

"He was pretty upset," Lauren responded.

Susan raised her eyebrows comically, laughing nervously.

"I guess so. I'd be upset, too, if I'd been sick for an hour."

Lauren hesitated, glancing at Chad. She was grateful that he understood her cue so accurately.

"If you ladies will excuse me," he said quietly, "I think I'll get a breath of fresh air."

Lauren nodded her thanks. But her eyes stayed mostly on Susan, who suddenly seemed very agitated. Chad was out the back door before she spoke.

"I'm sorry, Lauren. I really am. I know he ruined your evening." She started walking toward the stairs. "I'll go up and have a look at him."

"Susan, wait, please."

Susan stopped, but didn't turn toward her sister. Lauren continued.

"There's something I need to talk to you about . . . something Greg said while he was drunk . . . I didn't want to discuss it in front of Chad."

Susan seemed to suddenly steel herself. She turned and came back into the living room. She sat down.

"Okay," she began with obvious apprehension, "what did he say?"

Lauren took a deep breath. She had to talk to her sister about this, but she didn't want to upset Susan any further.

"I guess the best place to start is at the beginning," she sighed. "He was very upset that you weren't home. And quite frankly, Susan, I can't understand it either—especially since he's going away tomorrow."

Susan stared at her for a second. A lot of different emotions seemed to be passing through her eyes.

"Did he tell you why I went out tonight?" she finally asked.

Lauren shook her head. "He just said you go out whenever you want to."

Susan nodded, looking both reflective and sad. Then she got up and wandered over to the window. Lauren sensed the growing tension inside her sister.

"Listen, Susan," she said. "We don't have to talk about it now. It's been an upsetting night for everyone—I don't want to add to your problems."

There was a long silence. Then, by the sound of a small sniffle, Lauren was suddenly aware that Susan was crying. She hesitated a second. She couldn't ever remember seeing Susan cry before. Lauren walked slowly but surely toward her sister's slightly quivering frame.

"Susan, please. Don't cry. I'm sorry I said anything. It's really none of my business." She placed a hand on Susan's shoulder. Susan let it rest there a second, then moved away, going back to the couch.

"It's okay, Lauren. I just feel sick. . . . I can tell Greg has made you think poorly of me." She wiped her eyes, turning to face Lauren. "I don't know what all he said to you, but I do know he told Chad I was having an affair."

Lauren blushed very slightly but said nothing. Susan continued.

"I don't know what to say, Lauren. Our marriage isn't like most people's, because he's gone so much. I've formed my own group of friends—I've had to. I'd go crazy if I didn't. . . . The reason I went out tonight is that one of my friends is moving away—out west. I wanted to stay good-bye. I told Greg in the note that I wouldn't be late. He's just so suspicious. . . ." She placed her face in her hands. Another sob shook her. "Sometimes it just gets to me."

"I'm so sorry," Lauren exclaimed consolingly. "Maybe he was more vulnerable than usual since he was going away." But she didn't follow her instinct to go over to Susan; she had the distinct feeling Susan didn't want that.

"That's entirely up to him," Susan asserted somewhat angrily. "He could get a job that kept him home more. . . . But he likes to travel. There's only one thing that would make him change his mind...."

"A baby," Lauren said, more to herself than Susan.

Susan stood there a second longer, wrapped in her own thoughts.

"I don't even want to think about it anymore," she finally concluded, walking toward the stairs. "I'd better go up and pack for him or he'll never be ready to go." She paused on the bottom step, glancing back at Lauren. "I really am sorry you got involved in all this, Lauren. I just hope—"

"It's okay, Susan," Lauren interrupted. "Things like this happen. Don't worry about me at all. You've got enough on your mind."

"Yes... I guess I do" was the response, quiet and thoughtful.

"Susan? I don't mean to pry. Don't answer this unless you want to, but I don't understand why you stay with Greg. I can tell the relationship is really straining you."

Susan looked down. "Sometimes I ask myself the same question."

Then, without giving Lauren the chance to say anything else, she said good night and hurried up the stairs.

Lauren sat perfectly still, lost in thought. And she thought *she* had problems! They seemed very small indeed, compared to this complicated situation. Finally she stood up and headed for her room.

It was only after she was halfway up the stairs that she remembered Chad. She hesitated. He must still be out in the backyard. Her conscience told her she should go out and thank him for helping. Her heart told her no. She was tired—oh, so tired. It would be such a relief simply to continue walking, straight up to her bed. It would be good to close her eyes and forget all the confusion of the evening's events.

Yes, Chad had helped her, but he hadn't done anything extraordinary. After all, Greg was his brother, not hers. It wasn't as if he had been helping a stranger. And then there was something else. It was the way he had spoken to Susan. He had been putting pressure on her, subtle but very real pressure. It was obvious Susan felt very bad about Greg's condition. Why did Chad have to go out of his way to make her feel guilty? What right did he have?

If he was so sensitive to other people, surely he could have seen that Greg had pushed Susan into this situation. If her husband was never around, why shouldn't Susan enjoy the friendship of people who were? Especially after Greg had made it clear that he would only stay home if she were pregnant. That wasn't a deal, it was an insult. No wonder Susan had decided to form her own independent world. Greg had made it plentifully clear that her company alone wasn't enough to motivate him to stay.

But the more she thought about it, the more confused she got. She couldn't help but remember the unhappiness she had seen in Greg's eyes. He was really hurting, too. And, to top it all off, Chad wasn't helping either of them by blaming Susan. By taking Greg's side he was being irresponsible to both of them. No wonder Susan got fed up with him. No wonder she had warned Lauren not to believe a word he said. Her exasperation with Chad and the whole situation reached a peak.

There was no way she would go out and thank him. Knowing him, he'd probably planned on her doing just that. It would simply be another chance to get her alone. And why had he come home so early, anyway? Probably just looking for an opportunity to harass her. Fuming, she had just resumed her upward climb, when a voice interrupted her thoughts.

"I went for a walk. I was hoping I'd still find you up."

His voice was firm and clear, almost friendly. But Lauren didn't trust herself to turn around.

"I was just going to bed," she replied stonily.

"Could we talk for a moment?"

"I'm really very tired, Chad. Let's do it another time."

There was silence. Suddenly she could hear his footsteps on the stairs and a second later he was standing beside her. She could feel the heat of his body next to hers. A tingle ran up and down her spine; she found herself actually anticipating his touch. When it didn't come, she started walking again, first slowly, then faster. She had a chance to get away. She had told him she was tired. Why had she stayed there, when she heard him coming up? Why? It was as much as telling a man like Chad Bently that she wanted him to touch her—that she was waiting.

Her hand was on the door leading to the cupola, when his hand came down on top of it.

"Lauren," he said in a very steely tone, "I need to talk to you. It's important."

"Chad, I'm tired. Surely it can wait . . . this isn't the time or the place." She stopped, turning toward the door of Susan and Greg's bedroom. "I don't want to disturb them. I really don't."

"Then we have two choices," he said quietly as he took hold of her hand and spun her toward him. His dark eyes glistened. And she hated looking up into them. It reminded her of too many similar situations—situations that had been totally out of control. He continued, as if oblivious to the effect he was having on her.

"We can go to your room, or we can go to mine—you decide."

"Chad," she implored, "I've already decided. I don't want to talk now."

"You're creating an unnecessary fuss over nothing," he protested, opening the door to the cupola. "If anything will disturb Greg, it's us bickering in the hall."

"Chad, if we have to talk, let's go down to the living room."

"I don't want to be interrupted" was the icy reply.

"But I don't want to talk in my bedroom," Lauren exclaimed angrily.

"Would you rather talk in mine? Believe me, I'm being courteous. I think you'll feel more comfortable in your own room."

All the humor, all the understanding, had faded from his voice. He pushed her ahead of him, up the narrow flight of stairs. And she finally walked on her own only because she knew that, if she didn't, the result would cause embarrassing noise, and she'd end up having to explain it all to Susan.

When they reached the top of the stairs, a magical sight met their eyes. The small room was filled with golden moonlight; the black sky was so clear it seemed they could see every star in the galaxy. But Chad took no notice of it. She could see his eyes skim the room, as if casing it. Then he collapsed on the bed. He patted the place next to him.

"This is very comfortable. You're free to join me." There was just the glimmer of a smile on his lips. Lauren crossed her arms over her chest, leaning against the bureau.

"I wouldn't think of it," she replied coldly. "I couldn't imagine disturbing you. You seem so at home here."

"I am," he replied quietly. "I frequently sleep up here—that is, when there aren't other guests."

"Is that supposed to make me sleep better?" She made no attempt to hide the mockery in her voice. "The knowledge that you usually sleep in this bed?"

He laughed, a low throaty laugh. "I didn't know you had trouble sleeping, Lauren—but I'm not the least bit surprised."

"You have no right to talk to me like that," she snapped. "It's been a very upsetting evening. I want to go to bed. If you have something important to say, get it over with and leave me alone." Then, for some inexplicable reason, tears sprang to her eyes. She turned quickly away from him, so he wouldn't see. All she wanted was for him to leave. She just wanted to forget. The tears streamed down her cheeks.

There was a long silence. She was too upset to notice it. Then, suddenly, she felt a firm but gentle hand on her shoulder.

"Lauren," he said quietly, "what's the matter?"

Weakly, she pushed away from him, just as another flood of tears hit. She didn't want him to know she was crying, but by now there was no way she could hide it. And yes, very strangely, his closeness seemed reassuring. But she couldn't give in to the feeling. It was probably just because she was so upset. She started to step away again. Then, slowly but surely, his arms enveloped her, drawing her to his chest.

"Please go, Chad," she blurted through her tears, "I need to be alone." Yet all the time she spoke, she couldn't draw away from the firm, comforting feeling of his warm body.

He whispered in her ear, one hand stroking her hair, "I don't think you should be alone right now, Lauren. Tonight was more upsetting to you than I realized. I'm sorry if I added to it in any way."

She started to sob very audibly. He picked her up and set her gently down on the bed. A second later she was aware he was lying down beside her. A sudden sense of panic filled her. What was going on? She started to pull away. He reached out and stroked her cheek.

"Trust me, Lauren," he said very gently. "I'm not going to do anything to upset you."

Through her tears she could see his dark eyes scrutinizing her with real concern. And she did trust him. Somehow, she did believe him. She closed her eyes and allowed his strong arms to draw her near.

Time seemed to disappear. She didn't know how long they lay there. She didn't even know when she stopped crying. Suddenly, she was aware of staring out at the stars. It was only then that she realized she must have been asleep. Chad's hand was resting on her hip. She turned toward him, with sudden anxiety. Had he fallen asleep, too? What time was it? His eyes were wide open and he was staring at her, very calmly.

"You finally fell asleep," he said quietly, gently.

"I'm sorry," she stammered, feeling strangely embarrassed. "What time is it? I didn't mean to keep you up so late."

"I don't know what time it is. It doesn't matter. You took such a long time to get to sleep, I didn't want to disturb you."

"Didn't you sleep, too?" she exclaimed in a hushed tone, feeling flushed once again.

He just shook his head. Lauren sat up, feeling increasingly agitated. Her mind couldn't help rushing back to the evening's events.

"You wanted to talk to me about something important . . . before all this. The least I can do is listen to what you have to say . . . it was very thoughtful of you to . . . to help me." The words had threatened to stick in her throat. She was relieved to get them out, without another round of tears.

But Chad was silent. Finally, Lauren turned back to him.

"I really meant what I just said . . . all of it. . . ."

He was lying with his head on the pillow. His expression was very calm, very content. He looked more handsome than ever, with his hair slightly mussed. He gazed contemplatively at her.

"There were two things I wanted to say," he finally told her, barely above a whisper. "The first is that I wanted to thank you for helping Greg the way you did. I don't know many women who would have been so understanding." He paused, still gazing at her with his dark sparkling eyes. "And the second can wait until some other time," he finished quietly.

"If it's important . . ." Lauren protested.

Chad swung his legs over the side of the bed and stood up.

"Right now, it's not more important than your sleep. You've got work to do tomorrow—remember?" A faint smile played on his lips. Then he walked to the top of the narrow stairs. He glanced back, still smiling, and disappeared.

Lauren heard the door close, with mixed emotions. The events of the evening seemed more confusing now than they had before —except somehow she didn't feel nearly so strained, nearly so uncomfortable. She leaned back against the pillows, still able to feel the warmth of his body. She glanced at the clock. It was three in the morning. He had been there for five hours, just lying, watching her sleep. He hadn't tried anything, he hadn't pushed himself on her when he knew she was vulnerable. He had asked her to trust him and he had proved worthy of that trust. And . . . and his presence really had made her feel better. It really had. She smiled to herself.

After a few more minutes of contemplation she stood up and slipped out of her clothes. Seconds later she slipped between the cool sheets, a warm satisfied feeling filling her mind. She drifted quickly off into a deep sleep.

Sometime later, but before dawn, she was awakened by the sound of voices—arguing voices. Through the grogginess of sleep she imagined it sounded like Susan and, yes, strangely enough, Chad. What would they be doing talking . . . arguing, at this hour of the night? Pulling herself up in bed, she forced herself to wake up fully. But her efforts were greeted by absolute silence. There wasn't a sound in the house.

It must have been part of a dream, she thought. Probably some reenactment in her tired mind of the scene earlier in the evening. Anxiety crept over her, just remembering that. Without really thinking, she reached out to touch the side of the bed where Chad had been lying. He really had been there, she knew that. Even though the warmth of his body had long since dissipated, even though his strong arms were no longer comforting her, she could still feel his body next to hers, firm and sure.

And, as sleep started to descend once more, she felt a slow fire of desire burning throughout her body, a longing for his touch, a need to be near him. Once again she could feel the urgency of his kisses, his passionate words, his lips and hands slowly but surely arousing her, making her whole body yearn for more. And through it all she could hear his voice like an echo: "You can trust me . . . you can trust me. . . ." But just as his kisses streamed down her neck, closer to her breasts, just as she was about to abandon herself to him and to her quickened senses, Susan's image appeared. Her face was angry and hurt. She said nothing. And yet she sent Lauren a vivid message: Go away. That was what her very presence was saying. In her semiconscious state Lauren struggled to understand. And the more she struggled, the more she tried to pull away from Chad. But just when she was about to move out of his reach, the whole scene started over again, with the same intensity of passion.

It wasn't until dawn finally broke that Lauren slipped back into a deep dreamless sleep.

CHAPTER SEVEN

When Lauren arrived at the office the next morning, she felt remarkably refreshed and very determined: determined to go to Chad's office first thing and talk to him . . . about what, she wasn't even sure. And it didn't matter. She had awakened with the strange but clear feeling that she had misjudged him. How and why weren't questions she wanted to answer, just yet. They could wait till . . . and again, her mind stopped short. She didn't want to worry about details. She didn't want to worry about anything—not her past doubts, not her future hopes, nothing.

Jenny Wright wasn't at the receptionist's desk. Another girl, whose face was familiar, informed her that Mr. Bently was holding his weekly staff meeting. He'd be finished in an hour. Lauren felt a little anxious, but didn't allow that to dampen her spirits. An hour wasn't very long. She'd waited five years—for what? She knew, but part of her didn't want to admit it. She hurried to her office, to seek refuge in her work. That always made the time pass quickly.

On the way she passed George's office. He smiled, standing up to greet her.

"How about tonight, for you and Chad?" he said, advancing toward her. "I hate to let grass grow under my feet."

"It's great with me," she responded cheerfully. "Let me check with Chad."

"Good. I told Ellen I'd let her know by noon."

"I'll be sure to give you a definite answer by then."

He followed her into her office. She dropped her things on the desk.

"Are you ready to roll?" George glanced at the clock. It was only a little after nine.

"As ready as I'll ever be," she agreed, sitting down. "Do you have any coffee in that office of yours? I thought I spied a percolator there yesterday." She remembered with relief that Susan had apparently gone back to bed after Greg left. Though Lauren had missed not having a cup of coffee at home, she wasn't the least bit upset by not seeing Susan. She wasn't even sure why, since they had parted on friendly terms the last evening—she just wasn't sorry not to have to talk to her older sister.

George smiled devilishly. He reappeared, a minute later, carrying a foam cup. Lauren could tell as soon as she looked at it that the coffee was somewhat thicker than what she was accustomed to drinking. She glanced hesitantly at George and took a sip.

"This is, ah . . . marvelous," she remarked rather skeptically.

George seated himself with a satisfied look. "I knew you'd like it." He laughed. "Believe me when I tell you it really isn't five days old. That's just the way this particular Turkish coffee tastes, fresh. You'll never guess the name of it."

Lauren took another sip. It was odd but it did have a way of growing on you.

"You're right. I can't imagine what it's called."

"Black Gold—actually, that's what the Turkish translates to. Chad went to Turkey and Greece this spring. He brought me back a five-year supply of this stuff, because I usually take my coffee so strong. I hated it at first, but now I wouldn't drink anything else. That's why I bought the percolator."

Lauren laughed, enjoying the coffee more and more. It did sound just like Chad—at least like the Chad who had comforted her last night. The Chad she had just discovered.

A few minutes later the first candidate of the day arrived. Lauren was eager to get started, but she also kept an eye on the door. When she saw Chad walk to his office, she'd take a small break and go to see him.

But the time passed quickly and she didn't see Chad going into his office. She saw other staff members walking about, so she knew the meeting was over. Maybe he had stayed in the conference room to chat. It never occurred to her that he would have left without saying anything to her.

They had interviewed three of the six candidates, before George informed her they had a little time to attend to other matters. Lauren immediately took the opportunity to scout around. Chad was nowhere in sight. Everyone she asked gave her the same response. He had left the conference room, and then immediately left the office, without speaking to anyone. Confused and dejected, Lauren headed back to George's office. She leaned against the doorway.

"Do you know where Chad is? I was looking for him, so I could check about tonight."

George shrugged. "I thought he was supposed to be in, most of today. He had an appointment with the lawyer at ten, and then he had to go over the contracts for this new deal he's been working so hard on."

"Everyone tells me he left the office as soon as the staff meeting was over. He didn't tell anyone where he was going."

George leaned thoughtfully back in his chair. "I can't imagine where he's gone, Lauren. I know it was important that he go over those papers today. The whole presentation he has to make tomorrow depends on it."

"Well, I'm sure he'll be back, then," Lauren remarked quietly, having difficulty hiding her disappointment.

"Don't worry," George reassured her. "He'll be back and if he's not here by noon I'll just tell Ellen to assume you're coming. It's no big deal. We're used to cooking big, anyway."

Lauren forced herself to act as though George's reassurances were all she needed. But she returned to her work halfheartedly. They saw one more candidate before lunch. Lauren declined George's invitation to join him in the cafeteria. She remained in the office, hoping to catch Chad. When George returned, he came directly to her office.

"So," he said in a businesslike tone, "out of this morning's batch, who would you hire?"

For a second Lauren was slightly dismayed to have to focus

on work. But, as she started to think about it, she began to feel better. She needed a change of focus, and this morning's interviews had been an extremely useful learning experience. She and George discussed each candidate in depth, agreeing absolutely on their impressions. None of the four was quite right. There were either differences in philosophy, as there had been with Mr. Averol, or possible personality problems. In one case the woman's credentials were far better on paper than in the flesh. She hadn't had any practical experience, a reality that had come slowly to light during the interview.

They talked, totally absorbed, until the second-to-last candidate arrived. The woman was by far the most interesting yet—except that George finally claimed, when he and Lauren were alone again, the prerogative of simply not liking someone. He felt the woman was secretly antagonistic toward men. This comment was the first thing to bring Lauren temporarily out of the sadness slipping over her. She couldn't help laughing.

During the very last interview George was called to the phone. He excused himself, but came back only a minute later. After the gentleman had left, George rose to go.

"That was our fearless leader," he mentioned almost casually.

Lauren started. "Chad?" she responded.

"Yeah." George looked quizzically at her. "He says he's not sure about this evening. He wouldn't give me any explanation."

Lauren's heart beat very fast. This was one possibility she had never anticipated—never. What was going on? Maybe he had taken her more seriously than she realized. Maybe last night had convinced him she had meant what she said, instead of . . . Her head began to spin. What was she thinking? She wasn't even sure she knew what she wanted—except she didn't want him avoiding her. Now that her feelings were beginning to change, she had to know what his feelings were. She had to.

"Where is he?" she asked urgently, rising from her chair.

George laughed. "That's another funny thing. Our fearless leader, who is normally so totally dedicated to his work, has no intention of returning to the office today. And, quite frankly, I still can't believe where he told me he's going." He shook his head again.

"Not returning to the office?" Lauren repeated with increasing agitation. It seemed yet further proof that he didn't want to have anything more to do with her.

"He's going to the quarry, of all places. He called just to let me know."

"What's the quarry? Where is it?" Lauren pushed him.

"It's our own private swimming pool, just west of town. It's quite simply an old quarry. The water is very deep and very, very cold. Chad and I treat it to keep it clean. I just can't figure out what's going on with him. Why in God's name would he go to the quarry at a time like this? He wants me to go over the papers. He wants me to give the presentation tomorrow." Confusion had been replaced by incredulity.

"George, do you think he'd mind if I went out there to talk to him? I mean, he didn't say anything about not being disturbed, did he?"

"He seemed totally unconcerned about anything or anyone at the office. No, he didn't specifically say he didn't want to be interrupted."

"Draw me a map. I have to talk to him," Lauren said, pushing a pad and pencil into his hand.

"Okay," he remarked, obviously still confused. "But it's two thirty already. He might not even be there when you arrive. It's kind of a lonely place. I'm not sure he'd be too grateful to me for sending you there."

"I'm a big girl, George," she reassured him. "I take full responsibility for what I do—I really do." And as she spoke, she was thinking of the way she had let Chad stay and hold her. Yes, she had allowed him to comfort her—she had. And she took responsibility for that.

Half an hour later she was on a winding road, driving out of the city. It was densely lined with trees, but every now and then she could see farmhouses or open fields. Normally, she would have loved to pull over and admire the view. But the urgency of her trip wouldn't permit that. She had to get there as soon as possible. She wouldn't even allow herself to consider the possibility of his not being there. She so desperately needed to talk to him.

Finally, she pulled off onto what seemed like little more than a broken-up dirt path, called Smith's Road. The bumpy ride seemed to go on forever, but there was no way of speeding up. She knew that if she did, she'd knock the transmission out of her car. Ahead, on her left, she saw a huge pile of gravel. Her heart raced, as she recognized the marker George had told her to watch for. She turned off beside it, parking her car out of view of the road, as George had also warned her to do. She got out and looked around. The terrain was rugged—more bumpy ground, aggravated by lots of big rocks and thistles. She'd never seen such hugh thistles. Thousands of purple flowers dotted the land. She glanced down at her bare legs, wishing she had worn a pair of jeans. Her red cotton wrap dress was hardly appropriate garb for climbing rocks—and she'd clearly have to do that, to reach the quarry. She thought she could see the edge of it, and it was at least half a mile away.

It was only after she started her arduous walk that she glanced back to see if Chad's car was anywhere in sight. It wasn't. Her heart fell. Well, she'd come this far, she might as well have a look at the place. She continued on, growing less and less pleased by her surroundings.

Then finally, just ahead of her, she saw a small clearing, with several trees to one side. She hesitated a second. Was that movement? Someone seemed to be sitting by one of the trees. She scanned her desolate surroundings. If it wasn't Chad, she had placed herself in a very vulnerable position. There was nothing, no signs of any human habitation for miles in any direction. But if it was Chad . . . she sighed deeply and began walking.

"Hi," she said quietly. She had stopped about three feet away from him.

It was Chad, and he turned, with little or no surprise in his face. He was wearing nothing but black swimming trunks that hugged his hips very tightly. His broad chest was bare, showing a deep even tan that matched the color of his face. His hair was pushed straight back from swimming, its normal red highlights eliminated by the wetness. Water trickled down his face. He stared at her without smiling—in fact, it almost seemed as if there was a deep anger brewing in his dark sparkling eyes. Lauren suddenly wished she hadn't come. If the way he was looking at her was any indication of his feelings, she had just learned all she needed to know.

"I'm sorry," she said awkwardly. "I shouldn't have disturbed you. It's just that . . ." She paused, so unnerved by his expression that she momentarily forgot what she had planned to say.

"It's just that what?" he prompted her, his tone every bit as angry as his eyes.

Lauren stared, dumbfounded. No, she couldn't go through with this. It was a nightmare come true. The pain of being rejected, like this, after David, after everything that had happened . . . Yes, it was her own fault. She knew that. But that didn't mean she had to just stand there and let it happen. How could he look at her like this, after the tenderness of last night? What the hell was going on?

"I just wanted to thank you . . . thank you for your consideration last night. I can see you want to be alone." She had controlled the anger in her voice—but not very well. As she started to walk away, she closed her eyes, in a futile attempt to wipe his image from her mind. He had let her go without a word. Without so much as a good-bye.

"You surprise me, Lauren," his voice came after her, low and sure. She stopped dead in her tracks. "You came all the way out here, walked over all those rocks, scratched your legs on the thistles, all to tell me something—and now you're going to walk away without saying a thing."

"I already told you what I had to say—all I had to say," she protested, twirling angrily around to face him. "It's all too obvious that you want to be alone. Under the circumstances I'm doing the only gracious thing I can."

"How do you know I want to be alone?" he said sternly.

"How do I know you want to be alone?" Lauren exclaimed furiously. "Your expression, your eyes . . ."

"What do you really know about me, Lauren? Do you know me well enough to judge me by my expressions?"

"You certainly made no effort to keep me here," Lauren protested in exasperation. "If you'd wanted me to stay you could have told me, or—"

"Or run after you? Is that what you were going to say?"

Lauren felt her cheeks burning more hotly than ever. "No . . ." she began, totally flustered.

"Yes, it is, Lauren. There's just one problem. I'm tired of running after you. I'm not going to do it anymore. If you want something now, you're going to have to go for it."

His face was dead serious and yet there was just a twinkle, an infuriating twinkle, in his eyes. He had her, and she knew it! She clenched her fists.

"How dare you . . ."

"How dare I what, Lauren? How dare I force you to show your real feelings, after I've shown mine?"

"What real feelings have you shown me?" she demanded angrily. "You've taken advantage of me."

"Like last night?"

"That was an exception. It didn't mean much, not at all."

"It meant so little, in fact, that you felt it was worth a tremendous fuss just to thank me?"

Lauren shook her head, completely confused. "I meant, I didn't want to be rude. . . . I didn't want you to think I didn't appreciate it."

"That's not what you came out here to tell me, Lauren—and you know it."

Lauren stared at him. "Well, if you're so smart, then tell me what I did come out here to say," she finally demanded.

He shook his head. "I'm not going to do that, Lauren. You're going to say it yourself—'cause if you don't, you'll never be sure that I know. And I'll tell you something else. I don't have all afternoon to play games." He sat down on the grass, watching her intently.

Lauren looked down at her feet, as if willing them to move. At first they didn't. She only had to walk about fifteen feet to reach him, yet as she started toward him, it seemed like the longest distance she had ever traveled. He looked up at her as she stood directly in front of him. She realized how ridiculous it was for her simply to stand there. She sat down, facing him. Their eyes locked together, and for a long time she couldn't concentrate enough to speak. Being that close to him, especially when he was wearing so little, made her ache to reach out and touch him. But she could see he wouldn't break the silence. He would just wait for her—but not forever. She had to speak.

"You're right," she finally began, hesitantly, not taking her eyes off him. "I wanted to thank you for last night, but I also wanted to say . . . I mean tell you that I don't think I've been fair. . . . I think I misjudged you. . . ."

"So?" he responded, after studying her for a long time.

More blood rushed to her cheeks. "So!" she exclaimed, both from embarrassment and anger.

"So what does all this mean?" he pushed her.

Lauren sighed, more exasperated than ever before. He was demanding everything. He wouldn't give her anything—unless she gave everything. Once more all her doubts and hesitations passed quickly through her mind. They had all seemed so strong, so convincing—when she wasn't this close to him, when she didn't see the promise of passion in his eyes. When she didn't feel the warmth of his body inviting her to abandon herself completely to her senses, to enjoy the promise of what, truthfully, had indeed begun five years ago.

Her eyes drank in his body, so lithe and muscular. They scrutinized his expression—dark, serious, noncommittal . . . and yet, really none of those. There was something in his handsome features she couldn't capture in words. As if he understood exactly what she was considering, as if he could read her mind. Ultimately, she knew her pride was all that held her back. But her need proved too strong a competitor—her need to be loved, touched, caressed, her need to be a complete woman, a fulfilled woman.

Finally, it was the slow smile that crept across his face that forced her to action. That did it! The last thing she was going to allow him was the time to smile. In a swift, graceful motion she pushed herself to her knees, leaning toward him. Her hand hesitated ever so slightly before resting against his chest. The very touch of him filled her with more yearning than she had ever known she was capable of—a yearning, she knew in every fiber of her body, which she finally had to satisfy. She closed her eyes as their lips met.

She kissed him with all the accumulated passion of five years. At first he allowed her to do all the work, as if she had to convince him of her sincerity. Her lips and hands begged him for a fuller embrace. All pride and hesitation were gone, lost in the maelstrom of emotion. She felt no shame, only a complete, undeniable longing to have him love her as she had always wanted him to—though she had never been able to admit it.

And when he finally let his passion respond to hers, she felt no fear. What had overwhelmed her, in the past, now only seemed to fuel the insatiable hunger she felt. And the more her passion blossomed, the greater his became.

Lying on the soft bed of grass, he pressed her to him. His kisses strayed from her mouth with an urgency that threatened to devour her. His lips left a trail of fiery yearning, as they streamed down her neck. With one hand he opened the front of her dress. A second later he loosened the front hook of her bra. The lacy creation fell away. As his mouth drew nearer and nearer, the taut tips of her breasts arched toward him in uncontrollable passion. She felt his fingers stripping away her brief nylon panties. And, in mere moments, she knew full well he had shed his bathing suit.

His large firm hands roamed over her body, possessing it in a magic spell of unrelenting desire. Their demanding touch ignited and renewed her passion, until moans broke from her throat uncontrollably.

"Oh, Chad, I do need you, I want you," she cried, as his lips lingered on her belly, then slowly made their way toward the insides of her thighs. There, they nipped at the tender, sensitive skin, until she felt her soul would burst.

"Chad, please, I want you now," she pleaded, as his dark eyes glistened into hers. His hands cradled her breasts gently, lovingly. He kissed them for what must have been the hundredth time, then his burning lips met hers again. When he moved over her, his groan of pleasure, coupled with the feeling that he was, at last, totally hers, drove Lauren's passion to still further heights.

Then Chad stopped, for just a minute. His hand brushed her hair from her face. He stared into her yearning face, his eyes fiery and possessing.

"Darling," he said, his voice hoarse with passion, "I'm going to go very slow—I want this to be perfect for you."

Lauren couldn't answer; she couldn't move. She was filled with an aching love she had never before known. But she didn't have to think. Her body responded so fully to his movements, any possibility of mental coherence was totally blocked. Soon they were swept away together, oblivious to everything but each other, totally consumed in an intense throbbing that radiated to every pore of their bodies. The riot of sensation, the fiery release of love, seemed to last forever, cascading over Lauren again and again with increasing force. When it finally began to subside, it was only because her senses could no longer maintain the ultimate pitch of arousal. She slipped slowly into a state of euphoric exhaustion, exultant in her own body—and exultant in his.

They lay very quietly, for a long time, staring into each other's eyes, neither one speaking. Their breathing, which had been so quick, so intemperate, in the heat of passion, now came slowly, in silent testimony to their mutual satisfaction. Chad cradled her head on his arm. With his free hand he reached out to once again caress her breast.

"I'm incredibly glad you came out here to find me," he said, little above a whisper. His breath tingled pleasurably in her ear. She leaned toward him, allowing her breasts to rub against his chest, and kissed his mouth lightly but sensually.

"I have no defense. I was so foolish for so long," she finally responded, regretfully pulling away.

He laughed, a low throaty laugh. "I have no regrets, Lauren . . . darling. It was worth the wait."

"Really?" Her voice was a mixture of amusement and confusion. The events of the day had started to return to her. She shifted position, so her breasts were resting almost possessively on his chest. "Why were you angry at me, then?"

Chad looked puzzled.

"When I first got here," Lauren urged him. "You looked so angry."

"Oh, that," Chad remarked with quiet thoughtfulness. "I wasn't angry at you, believe me. I was fed up with you, but that's another story entirely. I don't think I'll ever be fed up with you again."

"Now that you've gotten what you wanted, eh?" she replied, amused.

"No, no. You're completely wrong, there. I've only gotten the beginning of what I wanted. It'll take a lot more than one treatment, even one like this, to keep me happy."

"Treatment? It seems I'm fated to be an angel of mercy." She laughed. "You know, you have skills in that department, too. You really helped me a lot after that experience with Greg last night. . . ." But her voice trailed off as she saw a dark expression reenter Chad's eyes. She thought it had begun at the mention of Greg's name. She hesitated, sorry she had brought any sad memories back. "Did I say something wrong?" she asked quietly.

"No, it's nothing," he quickly reassured her, running his fingers down her side, allowing them to linger on the firm roundness of her buttocks.

Lauren felt puzzled. His touch was arousing but it didn't block her mind completely, not now. She placed the tip of her index finger on his lips. "Why did you tell George you weren't going to go to dinner tonight?"

"I didn't think you wanted to," he said, pulling her closer, "and I knew you'd have a hard time saying no to George." A smile played on his lips. Lauren pulled herself fully on top of him, staring into his eyes.

"You're not telling the whole truth, and you know it," she exclaimed with a menacing smile.

"What do you propose to do about it?" He laughed.

"We're not leaving these terribly isolated surroundings until you tell me the whole truth and nothing but the truth."

"You're making me an offer I can't refuse," he moaned, softly pulling her mouth to his. "I don't think I'll ever confess anything, if this is the price I have to pay."

"Wait a second," Lauren said, laughing and trying to pull away. "First tell me and then—"

Chad grasped her firmly by the shoulders and pulled her back on top of him.

"Okay," he said after a long, moist kiss, "just this once, I'll tell you before I make you keep your promise. I couldn't bear the thought of having to be with you all evening, knowing I couldn't touch you."

"Well, what about last night?" Lauren exclaimed with surprise.

"If you knew what I went through last night," he said, smiling, their lips almost touching, "you'd never ask me to do that again."

"I never will," she responded, her voice growing weak with passion as their lips touched, first gently, then with growing urgency. They made love again, more slowly but with almost greater passion, exploring each other's bodies with increasing sensitivity. And yet, even as their love was again consummated, Lauren felt an emotional cloud hanging over them. She sensed that Chad was struggling with some worry, something that oppressed him. But the thought only filled her with greater love. When their passion was spent, she pulled his head to her breast and held him there.

He smiled sleepily.

"Let's just stay here," he whispered.

"We can't," Lauren replied, running her fingers through his hair. His hair was almost dry, now, and very soft to the touch.

"George," Chad said, nodding with resignation.

"I think he's pretty worried about you," she said quietly. "He couldn't believe you weren't coming back to the office. He couldn't believe you wanted him to do the presentation. . . ."

A smile flickered through Chad's eyes, then he jumped to his feet.

"Well, then," he said matter-of-factly, "I guess it's our responsibility to reassure him that I'm not losing my mind. Get dressed, woman, and let's split." Smiling, he threw her her dress. Then he stood there, admiring her nudity.

"What's the matter?" she asked jokingly.

"I knew you were beautiful, five years ago. I guess," he shrugged, "the more I see of you, the more I like."

Lauren laughed. "The feeling is mutual, Mr. Bently," she said, staring blatantly.

"Get your clothes on, or George will spend the entire evening thinking I really have lost my mind."

Lauren dressed, relaxed and easy. Chad carried her over the rocks and thistles, after making some humorous remarks about a threshhold. They agreed to drive separately to Susan and Greg's, then go together in Chad's car to George's.

The drive home, alone, filled Lauren with more of a longing to be with Chad. She reflected on the tenderness and caring he had displayed in their lovemaking. It was something she had never before experienced. And she couldn't help but compare Chad to David—except there was no comparison. Yes, she had loved David, she'd admired all his wonderful qualities—and they were many. But he had never, in three years, known her body as completely as Chad had in only one day.

So she replayed the scene of their loving over and over again, until finally she had to stop herself. Just thinking about it made her ache for his touch. And they were going to the Pattersons tonight, she reminded herself.

Chad was waiting for her when she arrived. It was after six; they decided not to bother going into the house. They were probably already late. Chad sped away in the waning rush-hour traffic. Half an hour later a very startled George Patterson greeted them at the door of his elegant split-level home in a very prosperous suburb.

"Where did you two come from? I'd given up hope." He laughed, stepping aside so they could enter.

Lauren blushed and glanced helplessly at Chad. She'd totally forgotten that they needed some plausible explanation for their whereabouts. Chad smiled very slightly.

"She dragged me out of quiet contemplation to discuss—of all things, business."

George raised his eyebrows in amazement. "Oh," he finally managed to say, "I had hoped it would have been something more interesting than that. You seemed so anxious to talk to him, Lauren. I somehow assumed it was more . . . personal?"

Lauren shook her head, relieved. "Just work, really, George."

"That's what women are like, George. All business—or hasn't twelve years of marriage taught you that?" Chad was wandering toward the back of the house as casually as if he lived there. Lauren could hear the amusement in his voice. But before George had a chance to respond, the three adults were descended upon by three screaming, laughing children.

"Chad," they seemed all to be calling in unison. His face broke into a large smile. He scooped the smallest of the children, a little girl who couldn't have been more than three, into his arms.

"How're you guys doing?" he exclaimed, with an enthusiasm that matched theirs.

"Great!" squealed the oldest, a boy.

The middle child, a girl, looked down at her feet. Chad reached out and pulled one of her pigtails.

"Hey, Laurie," he said in a quiet voice, "what's the matter?"

Laurie glanced angrily at her older brother. "Joel just broke the stove in our tree house. He came running in here, so Mommy wouldn't tell him off." The youngest girl burst into tears, and Chad whisked her up into his arms.

"It's okay, April," Chad said as he gave her a bear hug. "I think between your daddy and me, we can manage to fix the stove—in fact, we'll do it tonight."

"Dad," Joel exclaimed, fully confident that he had just been wronged, "I didn't do it on purpose. I mean it. I was just trying to lift up a chair, using a rope, and I tied it around the handle of the stove. . . ."

"That's not what happened," Laurie snapped as Chad set her

down. "You sat on the chair when it was in the air. . . ."

"Oh, come on, Laurie." Joel made a face at her. "I had to sit on it to test it."

Lauren, Chad, and George all had to stifle their laughs. Finally, George got his expression sufficiently composed to act the father again.

"Okay, let's cut this out, kids," he admonished the two older ones. "Joel, in the future, don't act without thinking. It sounds like you could've hurt yourself. And just be thankful you've got a handy father and a handy uncle. Now"—he paused, to be sure he had their attention—"I'm sure you haven't noticed, but Chad brought someone with him. Her name is Lauren. Why don't you all try introducing yourselves, eh?"

Just as little April was informing Lauren that she was going to have a little sister or brother, who would come out of Mommy's tummy, Ellen Patterson came in the back door, walking very slowly and looking very pregnant. She held one hand on the small of her back, but she smiled broadly and offered her other hand to Lauren.

"I'm so glad you were able to come, Lauren. George has said so many wonderful things about you." Then she smiled at Chad. He bent over and kissed her cheek.

"How's it going, Mama?" he kidded her.

"I hope not too much longer," she laughed. "That's why I wanted to have you over tonight. I wasn't sure I'd be home tomorrow night—I hope I'm not, as a matter of fact."

"I think you were very brave to invite us at all," Lauren responded gratefully. "It can't be easy, carrying that much extra weight and trying to run a household."

"Well"—Ellen sighed—"I'm not going to too much trouble. George volunteered to barbecue ribs. But if it had been anyone but you and Chad, I might not have agreed. George told me I had to meet you before you left—and once the baby's here, I have the feeling I'll have my hands full." She glanced at the older children, who were in the process of pulling an unresisting Chad out the back door. George was following after.

"Are they really going to fix the tree house tonight?" Lauren asked with a laugh, as George grabbed a hammer from the counter next to the door.

Ellen started to follow her husband. "You bet. The tree house was Chad's gift to the kids, last Christmas. He had one of the construction crews build it in their spare time. The children practically live in it. It's their favorite place."

"I can hardly wait to see it!" Lauren exclaimed. "I was quite the connoisseur of tree houses, when I was growing up."

They wandered out into the huge backyard, surrounded by bushes and equipped with swing sets, monkey bars—lots and lots of kiddy equipment. And the tree house was magnificent. It stood not too high off the ground, in a tough, gnarled old dogwood tree. Lauren climbed the ladder to see the carefully painted interior, with built-in cupboards and shelves. There were even built-in seats around a small table, so the kids could eat their lunch there. And when Lauren noticed shingles on the roof, she had to laugh. It was every child's dream.

The evening passed quickly, filled with numerous interruptions from the children. But it was fun and it was friendly. Lauren kept glancing at Chad, noticing how relaxed he was. He really did love children. Lauren could see it in the way Chad acted toward them—interested and attentive. Inevitably it reminded her of the time David had told her he felt children were unnecessary in a good marriage. She had neither agreed nor disagreed, simply because she was still wrapped up in her schooling and didn't really know what the future held.

Now, as she shared in this cheerful evening, her mind turned back to the subject. Her career was indeed very important. But sometime it would be nice to take time off. . . . Then she had to stop her mind from wandering any further. She was already planning a future that had absolutely no certainty. No matter what Chad had felt for her today, or any other day, in less than three weeks she would return to her home and to her commitment to teach. In all the passion and excitement of the day, that knowledge had slipped away from her. Now she forced herself to push it to the back of her mind. She didn't want to think about it. She really didn't. It raised too many difficult questions about

Chad, about herself, and about their relationship—questions she was entirely unsure could be answered to their mutual satisfaction.

This sudden realization, though she didn't dwell on it, cast something of a shadow on the rest of the evening. Lauren wasn't disappointed when, about ten o'clock, Chad looked at his watch. The kids were long since in bed, and Ellen was appearing distinctly fatigued.

"I think we'd better get going," Chad remarked easily. "We all have to go to work in the morning." Then he glanced at Ellen. "Including you. I don't know how you manage a pregnancy and three kids. You are one amazing woman!"

She laughed. "Women have been doing it for thousands of years, Chad. And they usually had the children closer together."

"I don't know how the human race survived, then. I'd be overwhelmed with a situation like this. And you do such a great job with each of them. They're lovely people."

"Thanks, Chad," Ellen responded, smiling at George. "Daddy's a pretty good executive assistant. Would you mind if I let George walk you to the door? I don't think love or money could get me out of this chair."

"Don't move a single muscle," Lauren reassured her. "And thanks so much for a lovely evening. It's been a long time since I enjoyed myself so much."

At the door George patted Chad on the back.

"Are you really sure you want me to do that presentation tomorrow? I know you didn't look over the particulars, but you already know a hell of a lot about it."

"Hey." Chad laughed. "I've hogged the limelight long enough. You go ahead and do it. It's high time the businessmen of Atlanta got to know you."

"I guess you're right. Once you've gone back to California, I'll be handling all this anyway."

"When do you return to California?" Lauren asked, with a sudden sense of shock. She had considered the demands of her own career, but managed to overlook the demands of Chad's.

"It's not definite yet," Chad replied quietly. "George and I just agreed in principle that he would stay here and run the office, and I'd return to California."

"Agreed?" George laughed. "Tell her the truth, Chad. We fought it out."

"You mean you both wanted to go back to California?" Lauren remarked, confused.

George shrugged. "That's where we're both from. But the reason Chad won out is that he's more mobile—and we think we're going to move our headquarters out of California, probably to Atlanta in fact, in about two years. I didn't want to drag the kids around. Or Ellen. It just wouldn't be fair."

"Oh," Lauren remarked, glancing down.

George laughed again. "Actually, Chad should be out of our hair pretty soon. He has to go back to the coast once this deal is all tied up."

"Won't *that* be a relief." Lauren tried desperately not to let her real disappointment show. Her brain had just gone into a tailspin. Luckily, minutes later, they were out in the cool evening air. They walked to Chad's car in silence. Lauren fought to keep a stiff upper lip, but she felt like crying. Chad started the car, then turned to her. He reached out and put his hand on the side of her head, sinking his long fingers into the soft hair.

"I know what you're upset about, Lauren." His voice was quiet and reassuring. "I can't tell you anything specific, but just trust me. I wouldn't let you down—I know how much you gave today. I don't take it for granted."

Lauren turned toward him and a single tear ran down her cheek. David, too, had told her to trust him. But she stared into Chad's eyes, knowing she had to believe him. He leaned over and kissed her, a long, slow, passionate kiss. It gave her hope, helping her to fight the sinking feeling deep in the pit of her stomach.

Back at home they found the house empty. But, out of courtesy to Susan, they agreed not to sleep together. Chad kissed her at the bottom of the stairs to the cupola. His last words, as she walked regretfully up, were "Trust me." She nodded ever so slightly, hopeful but not completely convinced.

When she was lying in bed, alone, she realized what a big

chance she had taken in allowing herself to love him—and be loved by him. Only time could tell if he was worthy of the trust he was asking of her—a trust that he had already gotten, in fact, because she had given herself to him. But how much time did either of them have? That was the real question. She fell asleep, torn between that thought and the memory of their lovemaking —her whole body once again yearning for his touch.

CHAPTER EIGHT

Lauren awoke suddenly the next morning. She started when she saw that the clock read eight A.M. How had she managed to oversleep? Her finger moved to the button on the clock, and the answer was immediately apparent. She had quite simply forgotten to set the alarm. She jumped out of bed faster than ever before. If she was to make the first interview at nine, she'd have to really hurry.

After a quick shower she rushed back up to her room, only to find that all she had to wear was the same outfit she'd worn the first day. She really did have to shop today. Downstairs she found the percolator full and a little note from Chad:

> See ya later,
> Love, Chad

She stuffed it into her pocket and took the time to gulp down a small cup. Where could Susan have gone so early? Or had she stayed out all night? What was going on there? Well, Susan could take care of herself.

Chad was waiting in her office, when she arrived. He made a big show of consulting his watch.

"My goodness"—his eyes twinkled at her—"my personnel manager is cutting it pretty close this morning. I was going to take her out for coffee, before we began our interviewing—it looks like we'll have to go to lunch instead."

Lauren smiled bewitchingly, sitting on the desk, just out of his reach.

"You can have the pleasure of my company for the interviews, Mr. Bently, but I have to go shopping at lunch. I'm running out of things to wear."

Chad leaned forward, a wicked grin on his face. "That's all the more reason why I shouldn't let you shop," he exclaimed.

Lauren leaned forward, so her nose was practically touching his. "Do you want me to come to work naked?" she whispered.

Chad feigned consternation. "On second thought, I think you should go shopping," he concluded, smiling anew. "But only on one condition."

"What's that?" Lauren laughed quietly.

"I get to go with you."

Her mouth very nearly dropped open. "Why do you have to go with me? I'm perfectly capable of picking out my own clothes."

"I know. But I have ulterior motives."

"What are you up to?"

"You'll have to take me along to find out." He grinned. "Now, sit in a chair and act like my personnel manager."

Lauren had just settled herself in her chair, when the first candidate, a woman named Priscilla Banks, was escorted in by Jenny Wright. She was about half an inch shorter than Lauren, blonder than Susan, with an hourglass figure even her business suit couldn't hide. Lauren couldn't help but notice the voracious look Ms. Banks gave Chad. And it bothered her to discover that she herself secretly scrutinized him, to see if he responded. Though there was absolutely no change in his expression and, in fact, he began the interview in very abrupt style, Lauren felt even worse, realizing that forty-eight hours ago this situation wouldn't have bothered her in the least. She wouldn't have cared if the woman had thrown herself at Chad—or would she have? she wondered. And she found herself wishing, with all her heart, that Ms. Banks had come yesterday, when George had been helping her.

But the interview went very quickly—much to Lauren's short-lived relief.

"So," she said, staring at Chad's handsome face, admiring his appearance even when he was dressed in casual work wear, "what did you think?"

Chad shook his head with a wry smile. "She's certainly not any dummy," he began, obviously still considering the issue.

"I agree," she remarked hurriedly, getting that same sinking feeling she'd had the night before.

"But there's something . . . I don't know exactly. . . ." His voice trailed off, almost as if he hadn't heard her.

"Do you think she's too assertive?" she remarked, trying to hide her hopeful tone.

"I don't know. You're very assertive, too, Lauren. But you don't come across the way she did. You're not trying to prove anything. You don't have to."

She felt herself relaxing again. It was comforting to hear him praise her.

"But on the other hand," he continued slowly, "maybe we'd better keep her on hold. She's a possibility, let's just put it that way."

They had three more interviews that morning. Lauren pulled herself together. She was a grown woman, not a teen-ager. She couldn't let a man take over her mind, and rule her heart, when she knew perfectly well they had no future together. She should enjoy the moment, and just forget the rest. That went completely against her nature, but after all she was the one who had started all this, five years ago. She was the one who had begged him to make love to her, five years ago. And she was the one who had gone out to the quarry yesterday, of her own free will.

She had to start acting like a responsible adult. If he was attracted to someone else, it was better she find out exactly what he was like, before the relationship went any further. Meanwhile, she forced herself to relax. And, ultimately, the work itself made it possible for her to do exactly that.

Chad was a tough interviewer, and a perceptive judge of people. She felt she was learning, just by listening to the imaginative questions he asked. They were simply ways of getting at ordinary information, and yet they never failed to tell much more than that about the individual answering them. She could understand why George had said anyone who could survive an interview with Chad would be able to work for the company.

But there was still another dimension to it all. He never failed to let her ask any questions she wanted to. That in itself wouldn't have been so stupendous. It was more the feeling that he did it very naturally. He was interested in her perceptions, even though it was very clear he could have done the whole thing on his own. Her mind went back to the academic situation. She had always thought it was the ideal place for women. There they really were respected for their intelligence, treated as equals, and all the rest. Being with Chad made her wonder. Her professors, and even some of her male peers, always made such a point of asking her opinion—as if to prove to themselves and to everyone else that they valued it. It was a small point, in many ways, and yet Lauren was amazed that she had never noticed the attitude before.

When the last candidate was gone, Chad leaned back in his seat and put his feet up on the desk. He seemed very thoughtful, very contemplative.

"A penny for your thoughts." Lauren smiled.

His eyes scrutinized her face for just a second, as if he were going to say something of real interest. Then he swung his legs down and stood up.

"Nothing that can't wait," he finally replied. "Come on. Let's go shopping."

"Don't you think we should leave separately?" she remarked humorously. "How would it look—"

"It would look just fine." Chad laughed. "You're not only my temporary personnel manager, but everyone also knows our families are related. Why shouldn't I take you to lunch?"

Lauren felt a vague sense of discomfort at the word "temporary." Chad hadn't used that word since . . . well, since he'd proposed the whole idea. Was he trying to remind her . . . or himself? Stop worrying, she admonished herself. In fact, she *was* there only temporarily. That was the truth—pure and simple. And it was her own choice. She was the one who wanted to teach. Not that she'd even looked for a job in business, to say

141

nothing of the fact that Chad hadn't asked her to be his permanent personnel manager. Actually, that was a good sign, since he had such strict ideas about not having romantic involvements with employees. And why was she even thinking like this? she wondered, getting increasingly confused.

"Oh, Mr. Bently," Jenny Wright's cheerful voice interrupted her. "Mr. Patterson called. He'll be back about one, and he said to tell you it went beautifully—better than he had hoped. He thinks the deal is all tied up. They might even sign the contracts this afternoon."

"That's fantastic news, Jenny. Couldn't imagine better news, as a matter of fact. I might be a little late, after lunch, but tell George not to worry. I'll be ready to go as soon as necessary."

As they stepped out onto the pavement, Chad put his arm around Lauren's shoulders—a casual gesture that nevertheless sent chills down her spine.

"I can't tell you how much this particular deal means to me," he said, his voice still brimming with enthusiasm.

Lauren felt strange indeed. She shared his excitement, and yet she also couldn't help thinking this brought them one step closer to . . . to his leaving. But she forced herself to forget her own concerns. This was a special moment for him, and he obviously wanted to share it.

"Chad, it's great. I'm so thrilled for you and George—for the whole company."

"Well, it's just that I don't think we've ever gotten a bigger contract. And we've also never worked so hard. It will make all sorts of things possible, in the long run. Most especially it'll make it possible for us to move our headquarters. I love California—I always will. But it's getting too crowded."

He guided her across the street and into a small but very expensive-looking boutique. But, once inside, it was apparent that their specialty was evening clothes. Lauren immediately turned to Chad.

"This is beautiful, but I don't need evening clothes," she said.

"Yes, you do," Chad said, leading her over to a particularly gorgeous creation in black lace and taffeta. "I think you'd look stunning in this and it's a six. Why don't you try it on?"

Lauren noticed the designer label at the neck, neatly but expensively apparent. She sighed, admiring the dress enormously, but unsure she could afford it.

"Who told you about this place?" she finally said, laughing.

"Susan," Chad answered immediately. "She's better than the Yellow Pages."

He didn't give her another moment to think. A young saleslady had approached. He handed her the dress.

"The lady would like to try this on," he remarked with almost casual authority. The saleslady smiled appreciatively, obviously pleased by his taste. She ushered Lauren back into a large, well-lighted fitting room. Minutes later the dress was floating down over her head. The effect was every bit as glamorous as Chad had predicted. The gown was waltz length. The fitted bodice and the top of the skirt were taffeta. But the huge flounce around the bottom was lace, and the sleeves and high neck were also lace. It was both innocent and alluring. Lauren took a minute to fix her hair, before she stepped out to show Chad.

He was sitting in an elegant armchair, patiently waiting. His eyes lit up.

"I don't see how you can live without it," he exclaimed, allowing his eyes to linger on the perfect way the bodice accented her high bust.

"I agree. But please tell me where I'm going to wear it? I have to have some excuse to spend this kind of money."

Chad rose, walking toward her. "This Saturday you're going to escort me to a black-tie civic function, which everybody who's anybody will attend. I decided it was about time I started appearing in society a little more—and now, with this new contract, I have all the more reason."

"Oh," Lauren responded, a little hesitantly.

"And also," he whispered, standing very close, "I haven't had anybody to take in the past—just in case you got it into your head to worry about whether or not you were being appreciated."

Lauren smiled shyly, then disappeared into the dressing room. When she reemerged with the dress, she was amazed at how readily she had decided to spend such an exorbitant amount on an evening gown. She brought it to the desk, resolutely avoiding eye contact with Chad. She wanted to pay for it herself. The saleslady smiled, placing it first on a hanger, then in a long zippered bag.

"You've made such an excellent choice," she murmured, handing it to Lauren. "And your husband is such a charming person."

Lauren started at this comment, then reached into her purse for a credit card.

"Thank you very much," she said quietly, handing the card to the saleslady, "but he's not my husband."

The saleslady stared at the card, then handed it right back.

"Well, then, your boyfriend is extremely generous. He's already paid for the dress."

Lauren turned furiously toward Chad, but he was no longer in the store. She saw him waiting just outside, his back to her. She thanked the saleslady once more and rushed out.

"Why did you pay for the dress?" she demanded.

Chad smiled. "I wanted to."

"But Chad," she insisted, "this is different. The dress is really expensive. It couldn't really be a gift—not yet."

He shrugged just a little impatiently. "If it bothers your conscience, just consider it payment for helping me." He was still smiling, but Lauren knew he didn't want to discuss the subject further. And neither did she. His last remark, in fact, had hurt her. They had never discussed the issue of payment. He had proposed that she take the temporary position, as a favor to him, and that was exactly as she had seen it. A favor pure and simple. The only thing she had hoped to gain from it, aside from the experience, was to prove to Chad that he meant nothing to her—and after yesterday, she had abandoned that notion forever. Whatever else happened, she knew she could never erase the memory of yesterday afternoon from her mind.

Once again she felt all her worries and concerns closing in on her, as she found herself futilely trying to consider apparently unanswerable questions about the future. Once again she started to feel herself being overwhelmed by uncertainties. It was only the firm pressure of Chad's hand on hers, as he guided her into another shop, that brought his words back to mind. She could still hear him saying "Trust me," and she forced herself to believe him.

With Chad along, the shopping went very quickly. Lauren was amused and pleased to see how quickly he gravitated toward the same things she would have chosen herself. And he was ruthless in his appraisals. He wanted her to wear only clothing that suited her to perfection. She ended up buying three outfits: two dresses, both of them silk, and a lightweight suit. And, much to her relief, he let her pay for them.

George greeted them on their return. "I think you're at last going to have some time alone in the office, Lauren," he said with a laugh. "I was just going to run these contracts back, so Chad wouldn't have to bother, and then Ellen called. She's in labor. I guess by the fourth time you know when it happens."

"Congratulations! Tell her I hope it was our stimulating company that brought it on." Chad slapped George on the back. "Forget about the office for a few days—but don't you dare forget to call us with the good news."

"That's wonderful, George," Lauren added. "I hope the labor is short."

George pulled out a Thermos. "I hope it's short, too. I've got daiquiris already mixed, and I don't know if I can wait too long to drink them."

He was out the door in no time. Chad walked Lauren back to her office.

"I don't know how long I'll be." He already sounded as though his mind were on the affairs of the afternoon. "If I'm not back by five, just go home. I'll meet you there as soon as I can."

Lauren smiled. "Who knows? If George and Ellen are lucky, by then I might even have some good news for you."

"We can hope." Chad started to walk away. Lauren disappeared into her office, but a second later he was back outside her door. "Here's the number I'll be at, in case you need me," he said, advancing toward her with a slip of paper. Their eyes met as their fingers touched. They gazed into each other's eyes for a minute, then Chad kicked the door firmly but silently shut with his foot and walked around the desk. He leaned over her, kissing her with a blatant possessiveness she could neither deny nor resist, his tongue sliding masterfully, assertively, as if to prove she was his. Lauren felt desire tingling relentlessly through her entire body, then focusing in the tips of her breasts as he crushed her to him. When he finally released her, his lips moved to her ear.

"I have a rule about making love in the office," he said huskily, one hand moving to cradle her breast. "But you won't get off so easily tonight."

Then he was gone, before she had the coherence to reply. The rest of the afternoon passed very slowly. She spent her time reading more resumés, setting up more interviews, and categorizing the candidates they had already interviewed in terms of who should be called back for a second interview. When she reached Ms. Banks's name, she hesitated only a second. Chad had said she was a possibility, and therefore she was. She wouldn't allow her emotions to interfere—but she couldn't help secretly wishing George would find something he didn't like about the woman.

By five o'clock there was still no sign of Chad. Lauren headed home. She had a strange, disoriented feeling, as if she sensed something were in the offing. Her desire for Chad was mingled with a strong sense of futility. And she had a sudden realization. She had to slow things down. For her own sanity, she had to. Tonight she would tell Chad that she couldn't let him make love to her—not again, not so soon. She had to have time to think. And the vivid, passionate memories his body gave hers blocked all possibility of thought.

This resolution gave her a partial feeling of release. She entered the house, not exactly cheerful, but at least with a sense of control. The first thing she heard was the light sound of footsteps upstairs. Then she noticed a purse, and an all-weather coat, on the floor by the door. Susan was obviously home, but it sounded as though she were in a distinct hurry. Strangely enough, Lauren hesitated before going upstairs. Maybe Susan wouldn't want to be bothered? But then she realized it would be rude for Susan to come down and just find her there. And that was when Lauren had to acknowledge she was afraid to go up. She really didn't want to see Susan—she felt guilty about her new relationship with Chad.

But that was crazy, she reassured herself. There was no way Susan could know about yesterday. She was busy with her own friends. She didn't have any idea what was going on. It would be rude and unfriendly not to go up and chat. She set down her bag.

"Hi," she said cheerfully, standing in the door of Susan and Greg's room. Susan glanced back at her, but Lauren couldn't read the look in her sister's eyes. What she did see very clearly was that Susan was packing a small suitcase. "Are you going away?" she asked, growing more uncomfortable each second.

"Yes. Just for a few days," Susan responded, her tone clearly indicating her unwillingness to discuss her plans.

"Oh," Lauren answered, turning to leave the room.

"I thought, since you were working, it wouldn't matter," Susan added.

Lauren stopped, looking thoughtful. "Of course. I'm not turning out to be much company."

There was another brief silence, then Susan spoke again.

"I hate to hurry off on you like this, but I have a seven o'clock flight."

Lauren followed Susan down the stairs.

"Are you going alone?"

There was a distinct silence, as though Susan resented the question. Then she seemed to reconsider. "With a friend," she finally replied, quietly.

Lauren felt extremely uncomfortable now, and struggled to change the subject. Susan was standing at the front door, as though waiting for someone. Lauren felt it would be impolite to

147

just walk away. Then something occurred to her. Her mind grasped at it thankfully.

"Would you mind just signing those papers before you go?" she said, confident she had struck on something neutral.

"What papers?" Susan responded, not bothering to turn around.

"The papers for Dad, the legal papers," Lauren reminded her, cheerfully.

There was yet another silence, this one embarrassingly longer than all the others. Lauren finally broke it.

"I guess this isn't the best time. I'm just afraid of forgetting."

"Well, there's no reason you can't drop them off to our lawyer," Susan responded. Her tone was casual and yet . . . and yet, there was a steely determination beneath the veneer of cordiality, a determination Lauren had long since come to identify as distinctly Susan's.

"Your lawyer." Lauren laughed very slightly. "But these are Daddy's papers. They were drawn up by his lawyer. You know what they're all about."

"Oh, it's nothing personal, Lauren." Susan glanced back. "I simply won't sign anything unless our lawyer has seen it. We use the same firm Chad's company uses. He'll know all about it. If you could drop the papers off, it would certainly make my life easier, as well as speed things up."

Lauren stared at the back of her sister's head in shocked silence. Then she got control of herself. Just because Susan hadn't mentioned this before didn't mean it wasn't indeed her policy. What did she know about Susan's procedures? And maybe it really was a good idea—it was just that this was different. This was her own father Susan was dealing with. Well, Susan had never been as close to their father as Lauren had. If this was the way she wanted to do it . . .

"Fine, I'll be happy to bring the papers over. I'll do it tomorrow."

"Thanks," Susan replied, her voice still slightly stiff and uncomfortable. Then she hurriedly bent over to pick up the coat and suitcase. "I've got to run now. I hope you and Chad enjoy the solitude." Her voice receded as she ran to the cab parked in front of the house, but Lauren was sure she heard more than a hint of unhappiness in the last remark—she was very sure, and it bothered her tremendously.

But she didn't have much time to consider the situation. She was just heading up the stairs with her evening dress, when she heard the back door open.

"Lauren, darling," Chad's voice rang through the hall. A second later he himself appeared, wearing a huge smile and carrying a large bouquet of red roses. Lauren couldn't repress her happiness at the sight of the beautiful flowers.

"They're gorgeous!" she exclaimed. But he didn't hand them to her. Instead, he placed them on a table and scooped Lauren into his arms. Their lips met, in a long, slow, passionate kiss that seemed to ignite desire in every fiber of her being. Every thought vanished from her mind, replaced by a burning sensation of oneness and warmth. When their lips did part, they stared into each other's eyes, wordless.

"I think I'm the luckiest man alive," he finally said, tracing a line down her cheek to her neck, allowing his fingers to brush against her breast. "Not only did I just have one of my biggest successes in business but . . . but I have someone very special to share it with."

A rush of love and warmth filled Lauren's heart, overwhelming her senses. Any resolve she had had to resist him melted away. All she wanted was to be his completely, forever wrapped in the fire of his passion. His dark eyes seemed to read her mind. He took her hand and led her upstairs to the cupola.

He laid her gently down on the bed, sitting down beside her. Slowly, and with infinite care, he began to undress her, stripping away each layer of clothing as if it were the petal of a rose, all the time looking for the precious bud at the very center.

By the time all was gone except for her thin bra and panties, she thought she would faint from anticipation. His touch was so light but so intense. She could hear his breath coming quicker, as was her own. All her memories of yesterday's lovemaking returned, making her weaker and weaker with passion.

"Oh, Chad." She gasped as his fingers worked their magic, massaging her tingling flesh and slipping seductively below the lacy band of her panties.

"Lauren . . . you're so beautiful," he said hoarsely. "I have to look at you slowly, to drink it all in. . . . I want to love you even more completely than I did yesterday. . . ."

Tears of passion and love sprang to Lauren's eyes. She couldn't answer him. He brushed them away, then carefully, so carefully, unhooked her bra. He leaned toward her, kissing the hardened tips of her breasts, rolling them tenderly but urgently between his lips until her excitement reached incredible peaks and passion burst forth from every pore.

He lay down beside her, slowly removing her panties. The feeling of his lithe, muscular body quickly rekindled her own desire. She leaned against his chest and with deft, anxious fingers undid the tiny buttons on his shirt. When her breasts rubbed against his bare chest, he pulled her mouth to his. Then his kisses strayed down her neck and across her breasts. When they reached the tender, soft skin of her belly, he paused, breathing very heavily, to remove the last of his clothing.

As Lauren looked at his naked body through the warm light of love, she felt he had never appeared so handsome, so irresistibly desirable. She reached up to him, catching him firmly by the shoulders. Again, his lips and fingers tantalized her eager body as her hands tried greedily to absorb every nuance of his body. Every place she touched was like a revelation. She wanted to know him as completely, as fully, as he seemed already to know her.

And when, at last, their mutual passion had reached undeniable heights and the thought of being separate beings was beyond possibility, he came to her, first slowly, then forcefully, driving her farther and farther up the winding spiral of ecstasy. The journey seemed endless, far beyond anything Lauren had ever imagined possible. Their desire was spent in one frenzied moment, but the bliss they savored in each other's arms seemed an eternity.

For a long time afterward they remained wrapped in each

other's arms, a physical symbol of the absolute unity they had shared. Finally Chad moved away and just lay there, staring into her eyes.

"Lauren," he said warmly, in hushed tones, "it's never been so wonderful for me. . . ." His voice trailed off as he allowed his fingers to brush the soft hair from her face, then move slowly down to cradle the soft weight of her breast.

"It was special," she whispered, still in awe of him and all that had happened. "So special."

He laughed very gently. "Isn't that what I told you five years ago? That you were special?"

She laughed lightly and nodded, drawing his hand to her cheek. "I knew even then what I was missing . . . when you stopped."

"I didn't want to hurt you." He kissed her cheek, still pink from the heat of passion. "And besides," he continued teasingly, "now that you're older, you can appreciate me more."

Lauren pushed him over on his back, resting her elbows on his chest, to hold him down.

"Oh, I would have appreciated you back then," she boasted, allowing a sly smile to play at the corners of her mouth, "but once would never have been enough. That's why I finally convinced myself you did the right thing."

He smiled back, but a more serious look filled his eyes. "I know I did the right thing," he said quietly. "I'm glad we waited till now. For all sorts of reasons . . ."

Lauren wanted desperately to ask him what the reasons were, but the tone of his voice somehow saddened her. It made her remember that she wouldn't always be with him, and she didn't want to think about that. Not now, not after all the beauty they had just shared. She didn't want to mix a drop of sadness in with that exquisite joy. She forced a smile to her lips.

"Well, I don't know about you, but I'm starting to feel hungry —after all that exercise."

He agreed, smiling, too.

"I think I could go for some great Italian food."

"Mamma mia!" she exclaimed with a grand gesture. "That sounds divine."

The drive to the restaurant was long, and during it Lauren thought about Susan's departure. She felt uneasy again. She wanted to tell Chad, she wanted to confide in him, but she didn't want to upset him. She'd mention it tomorrow morning. He hadn't seemed to notice Susan's absence at the house. It could wait.

The restaurant was huge, situated in the middle of a shopping center. Lauren's eyes widened. It just didn't look like the kind of place Chad would frequent. He laughed.

"I know what you're thinking. Everybody has the same reaction."

"It's just that it's so big."

"Wait till we get inside. Believe me, this place has the best food, and the atmosphere is a lot more intimate than you expect."

And it was incredible. She learned that it was owned by the brothers of one of the members of Chad's construction crew. The cooking was authentic and they even made their own spumoni ice cream. In the middle of dessert a crowd of people came in. They took a large table and, after a few minutes, one of them, a very tall woman with dark, dark hair, approached the table where Chad and Lauren were sitting. She smiled broadly at the two of them.

"Hi, Chad!" she said in a friendly tone.

He looked up, very surprised.

"Mary . . . Mary Bennett. Hi!" He turned back to Lauren. "This is one of Susan's close friends. Mary, this is Lauren McCloud, Susan's sister."

"Nice to meet you, Lauren," Mary remarked amicably. "I heard you were visiting for a few weeks. I'm sure Susan felt doubly bad about having to leave so suddenly with you here."

Lauren nodded, noticing a look of considerable dismay replacing the smile on Chad's face. "She'll only be gone a couple of days," she finally remarked.

Mary smiled. "Well, everybody needs to get away from time

to time. Listen. I've got to get back to my friends. It was good to meet you, Lauren. Nice to see you, Chad."

When she was gone, Lauren studied Chad's face. A mask seemed to have come over it. She couldn't tell what he was feeling, but he definitely seemed changed by worry or concern or maybe anger. Lauren decided she needed to do something to break the somber spell.

"I'm sorry I didn't tell you about Susan, Chad," she said quietly, reaching out to touch his hand. "She did leave rather suddenly. I planned to mention it tomorrow."

"It's okay, Lauren."

"I had the feeling it would upset you. And, since this was a big day for you . . . I guess I just didn't want anything to dampen your spirits."

They sat there in silence for several minutes.

"Did she say where she was going?" he finally pressed her.

"No . . . no, she didn't."

But the more she thought about the precipitateness of Susan's trip, and Chad's considerable unhappiness at the news, the more concerned she became. Then Susan's last remark came to mind. She had hoped that Lauren and Chad would enjoy the solitude. What could Susan possibly know about Lauren and Chad? Their relationship had changed only yesterday. Maybe she had guessed. That was a possibility. But why would that have made her run away? Granted, she didn't regard Chad very highly, but she certainly seemed mature enough to accept Lauren's point of view, even if she didn't agree with it.

Once in the car, Lauren tried to clear the air once again.

"Chad, is there something happening in Susan's life that I should know about? You seem so upset about her leaving."

He didn't reply for a moment, as though he were considering alternatives. Then he turned to her, putting his hand on her shoulder. He shook his head.

"No. I just get a little concerned about her, from time to time."

Lauren stared back into his dark eyes. "So do I," she replied after a lengthy silence.

When they reached the house, Lauren went up to take a bath. She thought she heard Chad make several calls but she wasn't sure. When she came out, wrapped in the scent of lilacs and her cool silky robe, he met her in the hall. His expression was serious.

"Sweetheart," he said, putting his arms around her and kissing her lightly on the lips, "I have to go to California for a couple of days. Maybe less, if I can manage it."

Lauren felt bewildered and then more concerned than ever. "Why so suddenly?"

"Just some business I have to take care of by myself." He gazed into her eyes and his expression grew visibly warmer. "Believe me, Lauren, I hate to leave you, I really do . . . and I wouldn't go unless it was very important."

She smiled softly, hesitant to let him go, but relieved by his reassurances.

"Okay," she responded quietly, gently stroking his cheek. "I'll take you to the airport in the morning."

He sighed. "I'd love that more than I can say, but unfortunately I have to leave tonight. That way, I can work all day tomorrow and get back sooner." He put his finger to her lips. "No, I won't let you drive me now. I'll take a cab."

"You're impossible!" she exclaimed quietly.

"No, I'm selfish. This way I can spend the trip imagining how beautiful you look in bed. If anything will hurry me home, that thought will."

They waited together for the cab to arrive. Though Lauren wasn't the least bit happy that he was leaving, she could easily understand the multitude of demands his company made on him. It wasn't until he kissed her good-bye and she saw more worry in his eyes that any other concern entered her mind.

"Lauren," he said, hurrying to the door, "I have to ask you to do me a very big favor. Don't get me wrong. I don't make a habit of asking people to lie."

"What are you talking about?" she responded, totally confused.

"If Greg calls in the next few days, please don't tell him Susan's away."

She glanced at the stairs, to avoid looking at him.

"Why, Chad?" she finally asked, skeptically. "If they're having marital problems, I don't think it's our business to interfere. I really don't."

She looked up, just in time to see him sigh heavily.

"Lauren, listen to me. It's not that simple—and even if it were, I'm not at liberty to discuss it. I made a promise I can't break. Not right now, anyway."

"Okay," she responded thoughtfully. "Okay."

She read the gratefulness in his eyes and couldn't help smiling.

"You'd better hurry," she urged him, "or that taxi will disappear."

He kissed her quickly, then ran out into the darkness. She watched him go with hopeful but questioning eyes. The evening had been more wonderful than anything she could have anticipated. She had felt both needed and wanted, loved and cherished. And yet . . . and yet now, she had doubts about something, she did not know what. Chad hadn't indicated that this trip had anything to do with Susan. In fact, how could it? He had no idea where she was. Then why had he suddenly started talking about her as he was going out the door?

She puzzled over that question for a good ten minutes, then grew very impatient with herself. Did she have to read hidden meanings into everything? Determined not to spend another second indulging this crazy line of thought, she decided to go upstairs to bed. There in the peace of her room she could remember the earlier part of the evening—the wonderful part of the evening.

But she hadn't reached the staircase before the phone started ringing. She cringed at the thought that it might be Greg, but she answered anyway.

"Lauren? Hi, it's George."

She sighed in relief. In the rush of the evening's events she had forgotten about the Pattersons' baby.

"Was it a boy or a girl?" she asked excitedly.

"A boy!" he exclaimed. "We started with one, and now we've temporarily ended with one."

"That's sensational! I'll be sure to tell Chad—"

"Hey, let me speak to him. Something occurred to me. . . ."

Lauren laughed. "I can't, George. He caught the ten o'clock flight to California."

"Whatever for?" George asked, laughing. But he sounded confused.

"I don't know exactly. He said some problem arose this afternoon. He didn't go into detail."

"He should have let me know. He usually does. I don't understand."

"I'm sure he just didn't want to bother you at a time like this," Lauren reassured him.

"Yeah, but I've just finished twelve ounces of the strongest daiquiris anyone ever tasted. I could handle anything, right now. I just don't get it, unless . . ."

"Unless what?" Lauren pushed him, only half jokingly.

"Ah, forget it. It's nothing, really. Okay, well, you tell the old bastard the good news, and I'll be talking to you at the office tomorrow. You sure got a sudden promotion, didn't you?"

Lauren laughed. "I didn't get promoted. I'm still personnel manager."

"Sure, but with both the big boys gone, you're now in charge. Or didn't Chad bother to tell you that significant detail?"

"No, as a matter of fact he didn't," she exclaimed incredulously. "But then, seriously, George, everything runs so smoothly at the office, I can't see the problem."

"Let's just hope no buildings collapse—I mean, none we've worked on." George laughed heartily, and Lauren joined him.

"Go and have some more daiquiris, and give my warm congratulations to Ellen. I'm so happy for the two of you."

"For sure. Get a good night's sleep. I'll be talking to you tomorrow."

Lauren hung up; she had just started up the stairs when the phone rang again. She continued walking, wondering all the time if she should bother to answer it. But it rang and rang, as if whoever was calling was determined to get an answer. Finally,

156

she couldn't let it ring another time. She picked up the receiver. At first there was only silence, interrupted by a lot of crackling. She knew at once it had to be Greg.

"Hello?" she called into the receiver. "Is this Greg?"

A second more of crackling and then it seemed to clear. She could hear someone's voice, but not what he was saying.

"Speak louder. I can't hear you."

"Is that you, Lauren?" the voice finally came over, faint but clear.

"Yes," she answered. "You might as well be in Timbuktu, for all the static on the line."

She heard the vague sound of a laugh. "This place is worse than Timbuktu."

"Did you want to talk to Susan?" Lauren decided to get it over with quickly.

"No" was the faint reply. "I know she wouldn't be home by now. I called to speak to you."

"I'm thrilled, Greg," she responded with heartfelt sincerity. "But why? It's not that I don't like to chat, but why would you go to all this trouble?"

There was a sudden outburst of static, so loud and so prolonged that Lauren almost hung up. But she didn't simply because she didn't know how long it had taken him to place the call. She didn't want to break the connection. Finally, it died down.

"Lauren, you still there?"

"Yes, I hope we don't get interrupted like that again."

"Listen, I'll make it short, so we won't have the chance to. I just wanted to apologize for getting so drunk. . . . I can't believe how kind you were. You should have just left me in there to suffer."

"Don't be silly," Lauren protested. "I understand."

"Well, that's the other thing I wanted to say. Don't worry about anything I told you in a drunken state. I was out of my mind. I shouldn't have been spilling my problems out at you. You don't get to see that much of Susan—I don't want to ruin your visit by making you think badly of her. I mean it, Lauren."

Lauren laughed from embarrassment. "I didn't take any of it too seriously," she finally responded, lying through her teeth. "It's easy to get carried away when you're not used to liquor."

There was a brief but poignant silence. Lauren wished with all her heart she hadn't made that last remark—it clearly indicated she and Susan had discussed the subject.

"Well, in any case . . ." Greg began.

"Don't worry about a thing, Greg. Please," she interrupted, trying to reassure him.

"I'm going to have to hang up. I really just wanted to apologize. Thanks again for being so understanding." He paused. "Tell Susan I called, and give her my love. Okay?"

"I will for sure. I'm glad you took the time. I felt badly that I didn't wake up in time to say good-bye."

She heard what sounded like a sad laugh, then more crackling and a very faint good-bye. She hung up, feeling slightly numb. She could still hear the hurt sound in Greg's subdued tone. She sighed wearily as she made her way up the stairs to the cupola.

She lay down on the bed. Then she laughed slightly, wondering how she could ever have imagined she'd be able to forget her own worries. And now that Chad was gone, his reassurances didn't seem quite so solid. Had it been the conversation with George, the one with Greg? Or was it simply the absolute silence of the house that made her feel suddenly so vulnerable? It wasn't simply that she couldn't give up her career, to make the relationship with Chad possible. She wouldn't give it up for any relationship. She'd worked too hard and too long. It was the strange but clear feeling that the past was somehow catching up with her. All those difficult questions had come back into focus. All the questions she had carefully thrown to the back—the very back of her mind—only yesterday, when she made the decision to drive to the quarry.

Those nagging questions had seemed buried, totally lost in the fiery passion of love. And yet, now, she knew she couldn't avoid them. Probably the answers weren't difficult. If Chad did love her, he wouldn't take offense. She had to know what had happened between Chad and Susan, however long ago. Lying alone in the dark, she knew very clearly that that single point, more than any of the other difficulties in her relationship with Chad, was blocking her from even considering a commitment—even though, so far, none had been openly asked of her.

And yet, against all the seemingly difficult problems, defying all rational, reasonable thought, was the memory of his touch—firm, knowing, and, yes, loving. She drifted off to sleep, determined to lose herself in work for the next few days. Neither Chad nor George had told her to cancel any of the interviews. She would proceed as planned. All her personal concerns were on hold, anyway. She wouldn't allow herself to sit around another second, worrying about it. She now knew what she had to do as soon as Chad returned, and she would do it. Whatever happened, happened. It was that simple.

And she would definitely make more of an effort to have a talk with Susan. She would begin by being honest about what had happened between herself and Chad. It was as good a place as any to begin; it would probably clear the air. As soon as Susan got back. She shouldn't be gone for too long. . . .

CHAPTER NINE

Lauren had just finished the last interview before lunch when Jenny Wright appeared in the doorway of her office, white-faced and stricken.

"Miss McCloud? One of the crew from Alvin Street is on the phone. There's been a terrible accident. I think you'd better speak to him."

Lauren reached for the receiver, shaking her head incredulously. "Of course," she murmured reassuringly to the pale young woman. "This is Miss McCloud speaking."

"The ambulance is here," a man spoke breathlessly into the phone. "It's Alfredo. . . . I think he lost his leg. . . . We don't know for sure. . . . The safety cable broke on the crane. . . . A big piece of metal fell. . . ."

"What hospital are they taking him to?" Lauren could tell by the man's failing voice he wasn't going to be coherent too much longer. She had to get what information she could out of him.

"Memorial . . . I think. . . ." A sob broke from the man's throat.

"Okay, someone will get over there," she reassured him. "Go and do what you can to help. Tell everyone to go home for the day—they'll be too upset to work."

Before she finished speaking, she heard the sound of an ambulance siren. Jenny was still standing there when she hung up.

"Did he really lose his le—" the receptionist couldn't finish. Her face had gotten whiter.

"I'm not sure, Jenny. Let's not jump to conclusions. I need to get in touch with Mr. Patterson."

"I'll get him on the phone." Jenny rushed from the office. Five minutes later Lauren was still waiting. Finally, she walked to the receptionist's desk. Jenny was just hanging up.

"Mr. Patterson can't come to the phone. There's something wrong with the baby. They just rushed him into surgery."

"My God," Lauren exclaimed. "Did they say what happened?"

"No. They wouldn't tell me anything. But it must be serious. He isn't even a day old."

"Okay, listen, Jenny. I'm going to have to go to Memorial Hospital. Draw me a map as quickly as you can. When you finish, look up Alfredo's file in my office and call his closest relative."

"He doesn't have any relatives here, Miss McCloud. He's from California. Mr. Bently brought him here."

"Well, call his next of kin in California." Lauren started back to her office.

"He doesn't have any relatives there. He's an orphan. Mr. Bently always took care of him."

Lauren put her hand on her forehead. "You'd better call Mr. Bently at the Sacramento office. He should know about the Pattersons' baby, too. And then you'd better try to reach the people I have interviews scheduled with this afternoon. Cancel them all. Tell them we'll have to reschedule for next week."

By the time Lauren was walking out of the office, it was very clear that the bad news had spread. She gathered from a few remarks she overheard that, at one point, Alfredo had worked in the office. No wonder everyone was upset. Apparently, they all knew him.

And the emergency room at Memorial was crowded with men from the construction site. Lauren had to push her way through to the desk. But just as she reached it, she heard several orderlies directing most of the men to leave. Only two were allowed to stay—a young man named James Ferrigan, whose right arm was badly cut, and Bob Bach, the assistant foreman. The latter was standing at the desk, telling them everything he knew about Alfredo.

"Who should be notified?" the nurse was asking.

"Mr. Bently, the president of the company, is his legal guardian—at least he was until Alfredo turned twenty-one. Yeah, I guess he's the one to notify."

"We've already taken care of calling him," Lauren said, stepping a little closer to the desk. Bob Bach turned to her.

"Is Mr. Patterson here?" His face was full of concern.

"No, I'm afraid not," Lauren responded. "His wife had a baby yesterday and there's a fairly serious problem with the child. We can't even get to talk to Mr. Patterson."

"And Mr. Bently's in California." The man sighed. "That's what Jenny told me."

"I'm afraid so, but I'm sure he'll come back the minute he hears."

Just then another ambulance pulled up. Lauren and Bob moved away from the desk, toward the waiting area. Bob pulled out a pack of cigarettes and offered one to Lauren. She declined.

"What happened?" she asked, after he had taken a few drags.

"The crane was just lowering one of those huge metal beams into place—the kind they use to support an underground garage. Everybody was clear. That's pretty standard. Then I looked up and the whole thing was wobbling, the whole arm of the crane. I knew right away what had happened. The next thing I knew there was a scream. It was Ferrigan. The metal thing was falling. It was gonna hit him. I don't know how Alfredo got there. He threw Ferrigan out of the way, then he tried to jump. His leg didn't quite make it." The man paused, shaking his head. "All the way up to the hip . . . if they save it, it'll be nothing short of a miracle."

Lauren closed her eyes, trying to erase the image his words had evoked. The thought of anyone suffering that much . . . it was too awful to contemplate. For a long time the two of them were absolutely silent. There wasn't anything to say. It was a waiting game. Alfredo was in surgery. They had a world-famous surgeon who specialized in reconstructing extensive bone damage, but . . . Lauren sighed. One of those metal beams must weigh several tons. Finally, she turned to Bob.

"Why don't you go home? I'll stay here and wait for Mr. Bently. He should be in sometime this evening."

Bob dropped what must have been his twentieth cigarette into the ashtray and rose.

"I guess there's no point to both of us sitting around. I just hate to leave."

"You've already done a lot, Bob. I'll call you and let you know what the surgeon says."

Bob stuffed his hands angrily into his pockets and shuffled his feet reluctantly.

"It's just that Alfredo's already been through so much. . . . I can't believe this would happen to him. He was so excited when Mr. Bently made him foreman. . . ." He took a few steps, then stopped. "But I guess that's why Mr. Bently did it. He knew Alfredo had guts. God, he sure had more guts than I would have. If I'd been foreman, Ferrigan would've been dead. I wouldn't have even tried to save him."

"You don't know, Bob. Maybe you would've. Don't be too hard on yourself."

Bob laughed, a tired angry laugh. "I really wanted the job—I mean, I wanted to be foreman. Mr. Bently said I wasn't ready yet. . . . I guess it doesn't matter. It's just that I was determined not to like Alfredo. And then we got to be good friends . . . close friends. I'd better be going. The wife will be scared half to death."

"I'll call you as soon as I know anything. I promise," Lauren called after him.

He stopped at the door and turned back. "Find out about Mr. Patterson's baby, too. I hope the little kid is all right."

Lauren nodded, wishing the same thing with all her might.

The hours wore on, moving more and more slowly. A couple of times she tried to reach George, but he still wasn't available. She called the office for the last time, just before everyone left.

"No, I haven't heard anything yet, Jenny. Tell everybody not to hold their breath. It'll be a long operation."

"We haven't heard from Mr. Patterson," the receptionist informed her. "But I reached Mrs. Patterson's sister. She's home with the three kids. Apparently the baby has a heart problem."

"Oh, no!" Lauren exclaimed. "They must be absolutely beside themselves."

"I guess," Jenny murmured, dismally. "They tried to correct it nonsurgically, this morning, but then his little heart started to fail. I sure hope this works."

"What did Mr. Bently say?" Lauren asked quietly.

There was a slight pause. Jenny seemed flustered.

"I completely forgot to tell you. I couldn't reach him anywhere. Not at his office there, not at home. The office manager said he was in for half an hour this morning, then left. He hasn't seen him since. He's been looking for him ever since I called, but he hasn't had any luck. Nobody knows where he is."

"Oh," Lauren finally responded, after a prolonged, thoughtful silence. "I thought he had urgent business out there."

"He did," Jenny answered. "Jim, the office manager, said they had a problem with some suppliers. But Mr. Bently took care of it in no time."

"Well," Lauren replied, a sinking feeling in her stomach, "I guess we'll just have to wait till he decides to contact us."

"Jim's going to keep on trying. He knows a lot of Mr. Bently's friends out there. He'll keep phoning around."

"I'm sure that's the best we can do. By the way, if George calls, don't tell him about Alfredo. It sounds as though he has his hands full."

"I agree one hundred percent. I didn't say a word to his sister-in-law."

Lauren hung up, returning to her seat in the waiting room. She started to worry about just where Chad was. But then she stopped herself. Wherever he was was where he most likely needed to be. She couldn't worry about it, especially when so many more important things were happening. When he did call, he would surely offer an explanation. The fact that the office manager didn't know his whereabouts meant nothing.

Afternoon disappeared into evening. And the evening dragged on. Lauren lost track of the time. When she finally did hear her name called, she glanced at the clock. It was already nine thirty. The surgeon met her at the desk, a mask around his neck.

"You're representing Alfredo's guardian?" he said quietly. She nodded. The surgeon started walking down a corridor, Lauren following. "Let me tell you, he's one tough fellow. I think he's going to make it."

Lauren heaved a huge sigh of relief. A faint smile broke across the doctor's weary face.

"That's exactly the way I feel," he said. "I didn't know what we were going to find. He's lucky to be alive."

"Did you save his leg?" Lauren asked, as they came to a halt in front of the door to the recovery room.

The surgeon nodded. "He'll have a long recovery period. But if he's lucky, I think he'll walk again."

He opened the door and they entered. Alfredo was lying unconscious, his leg in traction. She glanced inquiringly at the surgeon.

"How long will he be in traction?"

"Probably a solid seven weeks—maybe a little longer. The nurse told me you still haven't reached Mr. Bently?"

"No . . . no, we haven't," she responded, somewhat flustered. "I'm sure it won't be too much longer. He's out on the coast . . . business. . . ."

He shrugged. "Well, the situation is hardly urgent—that is, if you don't mind staying until he comes out of the anesthetic?"

"No, not at all. I'll stay as long as I'm needed."

"Such dedication," he remarked laughing. "You're only the temporary personnel manager, aren't you? I thought that was what I read on the card at the nurse's station."

She blushed slightly. "Mr. Bently is my brother-in-law."

"He's lucky to have such responsible relations. Anyway, I just like to have someone familiar around, when a person comes out of anesthetic. It makes the period of disorientation a little easier to handle."

"I understand," Lauren murmured, watching Alfredo's motionless body.

"In the long run," he continued quietly, "I suspect Alfredo

will have a few adjustments to make. He's obviously a very active young man. Recovery time can be very difficult—he'll start to feel like a caged animal. But don't worry about that now. You probably won't even be around by then. I'll talk to Mr. Bently. Alfredo will really need his support over the next few months."

Lauren nodded. "I'm sure he'll want to help as much as he can. . . ." And she couldn't help thinking that Chad would probably have to stay in Atlanta. Somehow that tiny piece of knowledge lightened her heart.

When the surgeon finally said good night, Lauren seated herself beside the bed. Her eyes were starting to get heavy. It had been a long day, and a very tense day. But it wouldn't take too much longer for Alfredo to wake up. She would wait. When he did start to stir, Lauren took his hand.

"Alfredo? It's me, Lauren, Miss McCloud."

His eyes focused on her face, but his face remained blank. Finally, he smiled, as though he had only just recognized her.

"What . . . what are you doing here? Where's Chad and Uncle George?"

"Chad's in California. We haven't even reached him yet. And George is with his wife. Their baby has a heart problem."

For a moment he looked very disappointed. Then he tried to move and his face contorted with pain. Lauren jumped up, grabbed a cool cloth, and wiped his forehead.

"I don't think you'd better move," she said softly. "The doctor says you're going to be in pain for several days—bad pain."

Alfredo tried to laugh, but once again his face contorted with pain. Lauren stayed right beside him, even when the nurse came in to check his vital signs and adjust the IV. When she left, he clutched at Lauren's hand.

"I don't need Bently anyway—if his work is so important to him. I'd much rather look at you."

She smiled. "Now, wait a second. I know he'll be back the minute he finds out. We just don't know where he is. I know you'd like to see him. I promise I'll get him here as soon as I can."

He closed his eyes for several minutes. "You know something?

I believe you," he finally responded dreamily. "I just want the big man to see where all his advice got me. He told me to set a good example—then everyone would work like a team."

Lauren squeezed his hand. "And they did. They all followed you to the hospital—every one of them. They had to be sent away. Bob Bach finally went home only because I told him to. That's the truth. They were all very upset."

"They were probably just acting . . . just wanted to get off work. You let them off for the rest of the day, didn't you?"

She nodded. "Was that wrong? They were so upset, I was afraid they might not concentrate."

"No, that was fine," he said after a long silence. "Chad and George would have done the same thing." Then he smiled. "But don't let them off tomorrow. Make sure they do twice as much. If they're so upset, they can prove it by pulling through for you. . . ." The smile faded from his lips and his eyes half closed. "I'm so tired. . . ." he whispered.

She stayed with him till he fell asleep. Then she drove home, through the dark, empty streets, her mind numb. She fell asleep as soon as she hit the bed, unable to think another second. It seemed as if only a minute had passed, when she opened her eyes to the sound of the phone ringing. The sun was shining brightly. She grabbed the receiver.

"Hello."

"Lauren, it's George. I'm still at the hospital. They just told me there'd been a lot of calls for me. What's going on?"

"Oh, nothing's going on, believe me, George. We were just upset about the baby. How's everything going?"

"We won't know for another forty-eight hours. It's pretty much touch and go."

Lauren sighed. "This must be agonizing. How's Ellen managing?"

"It's not easy for her. That's why I wanted to tell you I'll have to stay here all day." He paused. "We've been so lucky, up to this point. The other three were all so healthy. I guess what we need to do now is pray and hope."

"Well, please don't worry about anything at the office," Lauren reassured him. "I've got everything under control."

"Have you heard from Chad?"

"No . . . as a matter of fact we haven't. I guess he's very busy. When he does call, I'll be sure to tell him about the baby."

George laughed weakly. "It's odd he didn't call. I'm surprised he didn't want to know if it was a boy or a girl. Maybe I'll try calling him at the Sacramento office."

"He's not there," Lauren interrupted hastily. "He had to see some suppliers. I'm not sure where he is . . . I mean, not exactly."

"You really are on your own, then. I mean, running the office and all."

"You said it. But I can handle it. Don't worry."

"If you do need me, Lauren, leave a message here, and they'll tell me about the call. Don't hesitate."

"I'm sure everything will be just fine. Don't worry about a thing."

He hung up. She quickly got ready for work, thankful his call had awakened her. As she drove downtown, her mind went back to George's comment about Chad. It was indeed strange that he hadn't called, to find out about the baby. But if he was as busy with urgent business as he had indicated, it was possible that he'd forgotten. Unlikely, but it was possible. After all the excitement of the previous day she was in no mood to indulge herself by worrying about Chad. He hadn't said he would call and he hadn't called. It was no big deal.

Once she was in the office, she had no further opportunity for reflection. She was totally caught up with handling calls for Chad and George, running over to the hospital to cheer up Alfredo, and trying to keep everyone else working relatively calmly. She was just coming back into the office when she saw someone very familiar standing by Jenny's desk.

"Susan!" she exclaimed, unable to hide the surprise in her voice. "What are you doing here?"

"My plane landed about noon." Susan turned to face her sister. She was smiling but it was not a happy smile. She looked both tired and strained.

"Well," Lauren said, more cheerfully than she in fact felt, "I'm glad to see you. I wasn't expecting you back so soon."

"I guess you haven't had time to think about much. Jenny told me about all that's been happening."

Lauren sighed. "Alfredo's had a rough time. And the poor Patterson baby . . ."

"I'm sorry about Alfredo," Susan said quietly. "He used to come around quite a bit. . . ." But there was something in both her voice and her facial expression that made it very clear she was distracted.

"Susan, would you like to come back to my office for a cup of coffee?" Lauren asked with concern.

Susan laughed slightly. "Well, actually, the reason I came down here was to see if you wanted to have lunch. I had no idea you were so busy."

Lauren hesitated. Lunch was absolutely the last thing on her mind. Not only did she not feel hungry, but she didn't like to leave the office. She was in charge, after all, and today of all days she felt her presence was important.

On the other hand her mind couldn't help but return to her resolution to try harder with Susan. And not only was it clear Susan was trying, but it was also clear that she was upset. And she was seeking out Lauren. To turn her down now . . .

"I'd be happy to." She smiled. "It was sweet of you to come down to see me. You'll have to tell me about your trip."

"My car is just out front," Susan replied, as they got off the elevator.

"We could walk somewhere close," Lauren suggested. "Unless you have someplace special in mind."

"I thought we could eat at home. I've got a quiche in the oven."

Lauren felt slightly confused. Why should they eat at home? There were so many lovely restaurants downtown. It seemed a little strange, and yet Susan had obviously gone to a lot of trouble to make it possible. Maybe Susan just needed to be at home. What did it matter if it helped her to feel better?

"I can't believe you got off the plane, went home, and made a quiche!" Lauren exclaimed.

"Oh," Susan remarked, obviously flustered, "I didn't. I stopped at a good catering place. . . . I hope you don't mind eating at home, Lauren?" she asked, glancing at her sister for the first time since they had left the office.

"Not at all," Lauren replied.

"It's just that restaurants are so noisy and busy at this time of day."

But try though she did to sound cheerful, Susan seemed full of an almost palpable tension. Lauren's concern grew, but she hesitated to say anything until they were home. And when they walked into the dining room, Lauren was impressed to see how beautifully Susan had set the table.

"You shouldn't have gone to all this trouble, Susan!" she exclaimed. "It's beautiful."

A faint smile flickered across Susan's face as she hurried into the kitchen.

"It was no trouble at all. How many times do I get to have lunch with my sister?"

"I'm touched. I really am, Susan." Lauren smiled warmly.

Susan brought the quiche and a pitcher of iced tea. They both sat down.

"So, how was your trip?" Lauren asked, after taking a bite of the quiche. "Mmmm, this is scrumptious, Susan."

Susan kept her eyes on her plate for several minutes. Lauren started to feel awkward.

"If you'd rather not talk about it . . ." she began.

Another silence. Finally Susan looked up.

"Well, actually, Lauren, I wanted to talk about something else first."

"Fine," Lauren agreed. "What's on your mind?"

"I can't sign those papers."

Lauren stared blankly at her sister. "You mean Daddy's papers, Susan?" she asked, totally incredulous.

Susan stared at her sister another second. Then she lowered her eyes.

"That's right," she replied, and for the first time Lauren heard the snap of anger in Susan's voice. "I never had any intention of signing them."

These last words were spoken with such determination that Lauren set her fork on the plate and sat back in her chair.

"Susan," she began with real concern. "These are Daddy's papers. We're talking about his will. You don't want the farm. I don't understand."

"You never did understand, Lauren. And neither did Daddy. I don't think either of you even cared to try."

"Susan," Lauren implored, leaning toward her sister. But Susan steadfastly kept her eyes down. Lauren continued. "You know that's not the truth, Susan. Daddy and I love you very much. Daddy has wanted you to come home to visit for so long. . . ."

"Then why hasn't he ever asked me?" Susan demanded, her eyes glaring angrily at Lauren. "And why hasn't he ever come to see me? I have a big house. I told him so!"

"Susan, I'm not sure you understand how Daddy feels."

"And you do? Because he's always favored you over me? Because he's always confided in you?"

"No, Susan," Lauren replied, feeling more and more agitated. "I've always been around more than you."

"Don't you tell me 'no,' Lauren. You don't know what you're talking about!"

Lauren sat there, stunned into silence. "Maybe I don't know what you're talking about, Susan."

Susan shook her head. "If you don't, Lauren, it's only because you don't want to."

"That's not true!" Lauren replied, surprised at the hostility of her own response.

"Oh, really? Then try to explain why *you've* never invited me home or come down to see me?"

Lauren sighed. "Susan, Daddy and I thought you didn't want to be bothered with us. . . . We thought you didn't like to visit the farm. . . ."

Susan threw her napkin on the table, in obvious disgust. But there was a watery glaze over her eyes that betrayed her.

"You and Daddy thought! You and Daddy thought I didn't need my family!"

"Susan, I can explain," Lauren began imploringly.

"You can explain? Well, I wish you would explain why the two of you rejected me just because I wasn't 'quiet' and 'sensitive' like the two of you!" Two tears trickled slowly down Susan's cheeks. "I didn't blame you at first, Lauren. You were too young to understand that Daddy didn't much care for me. But then as you got older I began to understand. You took his side, naturally, because you were just like him. And then at my wedding . . . I understood how much you hated me. And you had never made any effort to get to know me!"

Susan burst into tears.

"Susan," Lauren pleaded, "I never hated you. Please believe me."

"I don't want to talk about it anymore," Susan answered, sobbing. "I'm tired of wondering what I did so wrong that I was pushed out of my own family."

"You were never pushed out. And I do want to get to know you," Lauren said quietly. "That was one of the reasons I came down."

Susan laughed scornfully through her tears. "Please, Lauren. Spare me the excuses. The only reason you came down was because you and Daddy needed something from me. Do you think you can fool me? Well, I realized that right away, and I decided I wasn't going to make your life any easier. Or Daddy's. Why should I? What have the two of you ever done to make my life easier?"

Lauren shook her head. "No, that's not true, Susan. I know it must seem that way to you. . . . And you are right. I didn't really try to understand you. It was easier for me not to see you, not to visit. . . . But then Daddy's heart attack made me realize how wrong I'd been. . . . I wanted to spend time with you. . . ."

Susan looked her sister right in the eyes. Her cheeks were still tearstained, but the tears had stopped.

"You wanted to spend time with me so badly that you took the job with Chad? Is that what you're trying to tell me?"

Lauren put her hand on her forehead.

"No, no, Susan. Please understand. That had nothing to do with you. I was trying to prove a point with him. . . . I was going to tell you all about it. I decided I *would* tell you as soon as you came back. I realized I'd been unfair to you. . . ."

"I think it's something of a coincidence that you should suddenly say all this right when I tell you I'm not going to sign the papers."

"Susan, I know I have been unfair to you. It isn't just words. I really am sorry, believe me."

Susan just shook her head. More tears welled up in her eyes.

"I can't believe you, Lauren. Words are cheap and I've been hurt too long. I thought there might be a chance when you first came down. But I can see there isn't! I'd like you to leave. Please go as soon as you can."

"Susan, let me explain about Chad. Our relationship has changed. It's very serious. I have to stay in Atlanta for the job and for him, at least temporarily."

Susan laughed through her tears. "You have a serious relationship with Chad Bently? Didn't I tell you not to believe a word he said? Well, I should have known better. You never listened to me."

"You'll have to talk to him, Susan. This is different. It really is serious. I know he annoys you but—"

"I already have talked to him!" Susan sounded both frustrated and angry.

Lauren shook her head in disbelief. "What are you talking about? He isn't here. When could you possibly have spoken to him?"

Susan stared at her sister. The silence seemed endless.

"I know he isn't here," she finally began. "I spoke to him when he came to meet me in California."

Lauren's mouth dropped slightly open. The whole inside of

her head started to surge in confusion. She kept remembering small fragments that now fit together. Chad's concern about Susan, George's surprise that Chad had gone, Chad asking her not to tell Greg that Susan was away, Jenny being unable to reach Chad . . . It all seemed to fit together. But it was incredible! How could Chad do such a thing—and after the way he had made love to her the very night he left?

"I can't believe that," she gasped. "I just can't."

"Believe what you like," Susan responded angrily. "It's the truth. And don't say I didn't warn you. Now, please, just leave. Right now. You've got no future with Chad Bently."

The phone rang. Lauren answered it automatically. It was the supervising nurse at the hospital. Could Lauren come right away? Alfredo was in a lot of pain and needed some encouragement.

She returned to the dining room. Susan was sitting with her elbows on the table. Her head was resting on her hands.

"I have to go to the hospital," Lauren said in a low, stunned tone. "As soon as I finish up there, I'll come back and pack my things."

Susan didn't turn to look at her sister. She didn't say a word. Lauren walked out of the house, feeling as though she had just been catapulted into a strange world where everything was backward and upside down. The only clear thought she had was that she should get to the hospital and help Alfredo. That was absolutely as far as her mind would let her think. She got into her car and began to drive, her face a blank mask, her heart frozen against the pain that threatened to overwhelm her.

CHAPTER TEN

Alfredo forced a smile to his strained face the moment Lauren entered the room.

"I knew . . . I knew you'd come," he said, panting a little. "Thanks."

Lauren took his outstretched hand, holding it tightly. As she stared at the tiny beads of sweat on his forehead, she started to come back to reality.

"Don't be silly, Alfredo," she said gently. "The least you deserve is a little company. The doctor says you're due for more medication any minute."

"Thank God!" he whispered. "I could sure use it. This pain is for the birds."

She rested against the bed, just holding his hand. They were both very quiet, but even after a very few minutes she could see her presence was helping.

"I'm sorry I didn't come back sooner." She made an attempt to sound cheerful. Her problems were not nearly as immediate as his—though a dull throbbing pain seemed to radiate throughout her body.

"If Bozo Bently would get back, you wouldn't have to be every place all at once. Haven't you heard from him yet?"

Lauren shook her head hurriedly. "No . . . I'm sure he'll be here soon, though. Don't worry."

Alfredo sighed, sinking a little farther back into the pillows.

"I can't figure this out," he finally said with a faint note of anxiousness in his voice. "It's not like him to disappear like this. Where did you say he went?"

"California," she answered. A renewed pain seemed to shoot through her. "Please don't worry, Alfredo. I'm sure he's just caught up in business."

Then she looked away. A minute or two passed. When she glanced back at him, he was staring very intently at her.

"Are you okay, Alfredo?"

"I was just going to ask you the same thing."

She nodded. "I'm fine . . . just a bit tired, that's all."

"I guess that's not too surprising. What is surprising is that Chad went away leaving you in charge and hasn't been in touch. . . . That's no way to treat anyone. He sure better have a good excuse."

"I can handle it, Alfredo. I don't want you worrying about me."

"Just promise me you'll give him a hard time, okay, Lauren? 'Cause I'm going to give him a hard time, too. He sure deserves it."

There was something in Alfredo's voice. Maybe it was just the way he seemed to assume that Chad did have a reasonable explanation for his whereabouts, or maybe it was just that Alfredo felt he had the right to give Chad a hard time, that brought a rush of doubts and fears to Lauren's heart. Almost before she realized it, tears were threatening. She didn't want to cry in front of Alfredo. She couldn't.

With a quick excuse she hurried out into the hall and straight for the ladies' room. She splashed water on her face. She told herself not to get so upset. She tried to convince herself that maybe there was some logical explanation. In the end she did manage to pull herself together, but she was far from convinced of anything except the anxious pain inside her heart.

She walked back to Alfredo's room. Then she stopped just outside the door. Was she mistaken or was that Chad's voice? She felt a strange mixture of fear and jubilation. She hadn't thought about what it would be like to see him again—not since the blow of Susan's news. But now she knew she had to. She pushed the door open.

"Lauren!" Chad exclaimed, rushing to her side. He slipped his arm easily around her shoulders. His firm body was warm and reassuring. "I can't believe what all has happened since I left. Alfredo just told me about the Pattersons' baby."

Lauren felt herself shivering. He sounded so concerned and so happy to see her—so genuinely happy.

"You tell him, Lauren," Alfredo said with a smug smile. "You tell him how hard it was for you. I just told him how ticked off I am."

Lauren laughed a little nervously. She could feel Chad's eyes on her, but somehow she couldn't meet his gaze.

"Let's just say it wasn't exactly boring."

"Oh, come on, Lauren," Alfredo pressed her. "Let's make him suffer. He has the most feeble excuse I've ever heard."

"Hey, lay off me, Alfredo," Chad chided him, laughing. But there was more than a note of anxiousness in his tone. His arm tightened very slightly around Lauren's shoulders. "I feel bad enough already. . . . Believe me. I know I've let you down, Alfredo. . . . I've let George and Ellen down, too . . . and I can see Lauren's been under too much strain." He paused, gently brushing a strand of hair from her forehead. "You look like you haven't slept since I left."

The intimacy in his tone was too much. She pulled very slightly away.

"I *am* a little tired, Chad," she said, and even she could hear the restraint in her voice. "But it's more from worry than lack of sleep."

"I told you, Chad," Alfredo started in again, "she's emotionally drained—and all because you didn't have the sense to call even once. Where were you and what were you doing that was so all-engrossing? Just tell me, will ya?"

"I told you I was in California."

"Then how come Lauren couldn't reach you at the office?"

There was a brief silence. Lauren stepped away from him. Now she felt able to look him right in the eyes. She had to.

"I had some business that took me away from the office . . . important business. . . ."

There was worry and concern in his eyes. He seemed very

177

fidgety. Lauren couldn't stand the tension another second. More doubts and fears had rushed into her mind. He was admitting something, but she didn't know what. She put her purse over her shoulder.

"What kind of important business?" Alfredo pushed.

Chad didn't answer. He just stood there, staring at Lauren.

"I think I'll leave you two alone," she said in a quiet voice.

"If you could wait another minute, Lauren, I'd be happy to take you home."

She shook her head. "You want to visit with Alfredo."

"Let her go, boss," Alfredo said. "She's exhausted."

But Chad didn't reply. He didn't say yes or no. Lauren stared at him, unable to understand what was going on, then turned and hurriedly left.

She forced herself to walk down the hospital corridor instead of running. The walk to the elevator seemed to take an eternity. As the doors opened, and she was just beginning to feel as though she'd escaped—though from what, she didn't know—Chad called after her. She almost decided to pretend she hadn't heard him, but in that moment of hesitation he broke into a run. He reached the elevator just in time to scoop her in with him. They rode down in silence. He took her hand as they stepped off.

"What's going on?" he asked, when they were out in the afternoon sun.

"I think maybe I should be the one asking you that question," was her slow, measured reply.

Several minutes passed in silence. They reached the car. As he opened the door for her, his hand rested on her shoulder.

"Lauren, you have every reason to be angry at me," he replied contritely. "I should have called. If I'd known what had happened, I would have come back immediately."

Anger welled up inside her, mixed in with all the other confused emotions. "What you were doing out there was so very important, but you could have left it at a moment's notice? Is that what you're trying to say, Chad?"

She turned to face him. He looked more confused than ever.

"It was very important, Lauren. Believe me. I'll explain it to you sometime. . . ."

Lauren stared at him in utter disbelief.

"I'm tired of waiting, Chad. Tell me now what you were doing in California."

He ran his fingers nervously through his hair.

"Lauren, the last thing I want to do is lie to you. I made a promise that I can't break. . . ."

"Did you go out to California to see Susan, Chad? Just answer me that one question." It seemed to burst out of her, propelled by frustration, exasperation, and fear. Now it hung in the air between them, with an almost palpable existence.

Chad stared at her and the confusion seemed to leave his face—but not the concern. He looked very upset.

"Then Susan was right," she said quietly, unable to believe her own words.

Suddenly there was anger in Chad's eyes. "Right about what?" he demanded. "What are you talking about?"

"Right about the fact that you went out to meet her in California!"

"She told you that?"

"Yes!"

"When?"

"She came down to the office and brought me home for lunch!" Tears had welled up in her eyes. All she wanted was to be left alone—and yet she didn't. She knew what she really wanted was—

"And you believed her?" Chad interrupted.

Suddenly, Lauren felt very confused. "You've just as much as admitted it!" she exclaimed, a little numbly.

He looked down and started to laugh, a mixture of humor and sadness.

"What's so funny?" she demanded.

His eyes met hers. He had stopped laughing.

"Well, I guess Susan's broken her side of the bargain, so I can break mine."

"What are you talking about?" she replied, totally mystified. "What bargain?"

Chad's face was suddenly very serious.

"I did go out to California to see Susan. But not for the reasons you or anyone else might imagine."

"Then why . . ." Lauren began.

Chad placed his hand on her shoulder. He looked very uncomfortable. He shook his head.

"I'm not sure where to begin," he said slowly. "I guess the first thing to say is that Susan hasn't been very happy with Greg. I think she married him for the wrong reasons. And, in all honesty, as much as I love my brother, he has some growing up to do." He paused, as if trying to sort out the sequence of facts. "They probably would have parted a long time ago, if Susan didn't happen to be a very loyal person. She chose to marry him and she felt very responsible for that. If she were to let the marriage fail without really working at it . . . it would have been against her nature."

Lauren shook her head in confusion.

"Well, how do you fit in, Chad?"

He laughed skeptically.

"I guess I just kind of stumbled in. When Greg and Susan moved to Atlanta, they were starting to have very serious problems. Greg asked me to stay at the house when I was in town to keep Susan company, he was away so much . . . and then, Susan started to confide in me a bit. She doesn't open up to people easily, I'm sure that's no news to you. I guess we became friends. I think I'm one of the few people she really trusts."

"That doesn't make any sense," Lauren said, bewildered. "One of the first things she said to me was that I shouldn't believe a word you said!"

He sighed. "Well, that doesn't reflect on me so much as it does on your relationship with her."

"I don't really understand."

"I don't think Susan wanted you to get close to me, because she was afraid you'd find out about her problems. She's very proud—and I think she's felt threatened by you for a long time."

Lauren nodded. "That's basically what she was upset about at lunch."

"And, I think there's probably also a small element of jealousy.... I don't think she wanted you to have a relationship with me."

Lauren felt her cheeks getting warm. All her memories of Susan's wedding came rushing back.

"Chad," she began, very tentatively, "was there ever anything between you and Susan?"

He smiled and shook his head. "No."

"Then why was she fussing over you so much at the wedding?"

"When I met Susan, she was already engaged to my brother. But even if she hadn't been... I don't know how to say it except that she just wasn't my type. I think that, for a while, she wished I felt differently."

Lauren sighed with relief. A slow smile crept across her face. She reached out and took Chad's hand.

"So why did you follow her to California? How did you even know she was going there?"

"One of Susan's friends is a man named Alex Vorst. He's an airline pilot. He's the fellow she went to dinner with the night Greg got drunk. Anyway, he got transferred to Los Angeles. He's been trying to start something up with Susan for some time. Up until dinner that night she wasn't interested."

"What happened then?"

Chad sighed. "She was still up at three o'clock in the morning, when I came down from your room.... She was angry at Greg and fed up because she felt her life was going nowhere. And, naturally, she assumed what was, in fact, the truth about us—although you wouldn't admit it yet.... I guess seeing you and all that you'd done with your life reminded her of her own inadequacies. We started to talk and it turned into a big argument."

"I thought I heard you and Susan arguing, but I assumed it was all part of a dream."

"I wish it had been. I told her that I loved you... that it was just a matter of time before you realized you felt the same way for me. She flew off the handle, saying she was sick of trying with Greg and that Alex had suggested she come to Los Angeles and live with him. . . . I told her if she did take him up on it, it would be the worst mistake she'd ever made. . . . We parted angrily. That was why I left the office, the next morning, right after the meeting. She had been asleep when I had left, and I wanted to talk to her some more. . . . She seemed more reasonable, though she was still very upset. . . . I started to worry about the ramifications it all might have for the future of our relationship."

Lauren smiled lovingly. She stroked his cheek. "So that was why you went out to the quarry."

"I was afraid of causing any more tension between the two of you—but then when you came out . . . Let's just say you made up my mind for me. . . ."

He put his arms around her and drew her tightly to his chest. His lips met hers with a slow, easy kiss that kindled her passion very subtly but surely. When he drew away, they stayed with their arms around each other.

"I realized that what we had together was even more special than I had ever realized. . . . I was determined I would hold on to you, no matter what. That was why I had to go to California—to try to convince Susan not to hurt herself or us. . . ."

"Did you know she had come back?" Lauren asked, very confused.

He shook his head. "When I left her, she was determined to stay. Vorst was away, so nothing much could have happened between them. I guess that night she did a lot of thinking. I'm really sorry she hurt you as much as she did, Lauren."

Lauren's mind and heart were filled with concern. She looked down.

"There's a lot I don't understand about Susan, Chad, but she was right at lunch today when she said I'd never made any real effort to get to know her. And now all of this . . . at least some of it is my fault, Chad. I'm ashamed to admit it, but that is the truth."

Chad put his fingers under her chin. He tipped her face toward his.

"That's a good place to start, Lauren. I think Susan is very confused and very unhappy. She really needs her family."

Lauren nodded. "When I left her to come to the hospital, I wasn't sure she'd ever speak to me again. I'd like to go home. . . . I'd like to see what we can resolve. . . ."

When they reached the house, it was completely quiet. Lauren looked all around the first floor and was just starting up the stairs when the door to Greg and Susan's bedroom opened. Susan emerged with a tear-streaked face. At first she didn't see Lauren. When she did notice her, Susan's face filled with surprise.

"I didn't mean to sneak up on you," Lauren began apologetically. She glanced back at the living room. Chad was sitting there. Susan's eyes followed Lauren's. She didn't say a word.

"Susan, can we talk a little more?" Lauren asked tentatively

"I . . . I don't know. What's there to talk about?"

Lauren finished climbing the stairs.

"I've been talking to Chad about a lot of things, Susan. You were right. I think I've been very unfair to you. I'm sorry."

Susan leaned back against the wall. Confusion and then amazement filled her eyes. More tears started to roll down her cheeks.

"You mean, you're not angry at me for what I said about me and Chad?" she said through her tears. "And Chad's not angry?"

Lauren shook her head.

"No, Susan. I think we really do understand what you were going through. . . . Maybe you and I could learn to trust each other more. . . ."

Susan started to cry harder. Lauren put her arm around her sister's shoulders. Susan didn't move away.

"It wasn't all your fault, Lauren," Susan cried. "I felt sick after you left. I know Chad loves you. I was worried that when you found out the truth you'd never speak to me again. . . . I was just so angry. I didn't mean to hurt you so much. . . ."

"It's okay, Susan," Lauren reassured her. "I guess I've hurt you, too, over the years. Believe me, I didn't mean it, either."

"I just don't know what I'm going to do," Susan went on, sobbing. "I don't know if I can stay with Greg . . . so much has happened. . . ."

"Don't rush into any decision, Susan. You can take as much time as you need. I'll do anything I can to help you."

Finally, Susan stopped crying. She walked over to look in the mirror on the wall. Then she laughed.

"The beautiful Susan Bently," she said, making a face.

"All you need is some cold water and a rest," Lauren suggested.

Susan turned to face her sister. "You're right, Lauren," she said, sighing wearily. "I do need some rest. I haven't slept in three days. . . . I've been so worried about everything. . . ."

"Why don't you lie down now? Chad and I have to go and see the Pattersons."

"Oh." Susan suddenly remembered. "George called just after you left. I was so upset, I forgot to tell you. The baby's going to be all right."

"My God!" Lauren sighed with relief. "That's wonderful. Chad will be so thrilled. You rest, Susan, then maybe we can all go out to dinner later."

Susan nodded, a little numbly. "Fine, I'll be ready."

Lauren smiled, then started to walk away.

"And Lauren," Susan called after her, "thanks for coming back. . . . I'm not sure what I would've done if you hadn't. I'd like us to be friends."

Lauren went back and hugged her sister warmly. "Me, too. And Susan, don't judge Daddy too harshly. He really does love you. I think he was afraid you didn't love him. It's awfully hard for him to talk about his feelings."

Susan nodded. "I think I have a lot of bridge mending to do."

"Chad and I are going to go home and see Daddy, when I finish up at the company. You're more than welcome to come with us. I think Daddy would be very pleased to see you."

"I don't know," Susan said thoughtfully. "But maybe it would be a good idea. I need some time to think . . . and the farm really is such a quiet place."

"I'd love to have you come along, and so would Chad."

"Did I hear you say we were going to see your father after you finished up at the company?" Chad said very casually, late that night, when they were lying in each other's arms, bathed in the moonlight streaming into the cupola. Susan had gone to visit Mary Bennett.

Lauren laughed. "Of course. Isn't that what we agreed?"

Chad raised himself on his elbow and stared down into her eyes.

"I said we would go in two weeks."

"Well, that's when I finish," she protested.

He shook his head, looking very serious. "I was hoping you'd agree to stay on—permanently."

Lauren pulled herself up so that she was leaning against the headboard.

"Wait a second," she said, laughing with amazement. "We haven't talked about anything that far in the future. What about my teaching position?"

"You'll have to make that decision for yourself." He grinned. "From what you've already told me, I'm offering you the first real alternative to teaching you've had. What do you think?"

Lauren sat there thoughtfully. A few minutes passed in silence, then a sly smile crept across her face.

"Well, it's a tempting offer. I think working for Suncon is very exciting, but . . ."

"But what?" he pressed her, a slight anxiousness filling his eyes.

"If I'm not mistaken, you have a company policy. You don't like to be romantically involved with employees."

"Oh, that!" he exclaimed. "I don't see how that could possibly be a consideration—you wouldn't be an employee."

"Chad Bently, what in God's name are you talking about?"

He shrugged nonchalantly. "I'm talking about the fact that, as my wife, you'd be a partner in the business."

"As your wife!" She laughed incredulously. "Aren't you assuming an awful lot? You haven't even asked me."

He stared at her a second, then slowly started to pull her down beside him. His lips hovered tantalizingly above hers. His hands roamed over her bare flesh teasingly, awakening her desire at their will. But before the two of them abandoned themselves totally to the delirium of love, she had answered yes to all his questions.

LOOK FOR NEXT MONTH'S
CANDLELIGHT ECSTASY ROMANCES ®

186 GEMSTONE, *Bonnie Drake*
187 A TIME TO LOVE, *Jackie Black*
188 WINDSONG, *Jo Calloway*
189 LOVE'S MADNESS, *Sheila Paulos*
190 DESTINY'S TOUCH, *Dorothy Ann Bernard*
191 NO OTHER LOVE, *Alyssa Morgan*
192 THE DEDICATED MAN, *Lass Small*
193 MEMORY AND DESIRE, *Eileen Bryan*

When You Want A Little More Than Romance—

Try A Candlelight Ecstasy!

Dell — **Wherever paperback books are sold!**

NEW DELL

Candlelight Ecstasy Supreme

TEMPESTUOUS EDEN,
by Heather Graham.
$2.50

Blair Morgan—daughter of a powerful man, widow of a famous senator—sacrifices a world of wealth to work among the needy in the Central American jungle and meets Craig Taylor, a man she can deny nothing.

EMERALD FIRE,
by Barbara Andrews
$2.50

She was stranded on a deserted island with a handsome millionaire—what more could Kelly want? Love.

THE SEEDS OF SINGING
by Kay McGrath

To the primitive tribes of New Guinea, the seeds of singing are the essence of courage. To Michael Stanford and Catherine Morgan, two young explorers on a lost expedition, they symbolize a passion that defies war, separation, and time itself. In the unmapped highlands beyond the jungle, in a world untouched since the dawn of time, Michael and Catherine discover a passion men and women everywhere only dream about, a love that will outlast everything.

A DELL BOOK   19120-3 $3.95

At your local bookstore or use this handy coupon for ordering:

Dell   DELL BOOKS   THE SEEDS OF SINGING   19120-3 $3.95
P.O. BOX 1000, PINE BROOK, N.J. 07058-1000

Please send me the above title. I am enclosing $_____ (please add 75c per copy to cover postage and handling). Send check or money order—no cash or C.O.D.'s. Please allow up to 8 weeks for shipment.

Name _____

Address _____

City _____ State/Zip _____

NEW DELL

Candlelight Ecstasy Supreme

LOVERS AND PRETENDERS,
by Prudence Martin
$2.50

Christine and Paul—looking for new lives on a cross-country jaunt, were bound by lies and a passion that grew more dangerously honest with each passing day. Would the truth destroy their love?

WARMED BY THE FIRE,
by Donna Kimel Vitek
$2.50

When malicious gossip forces Juliet to switch jobs from one television network to another, she swears an office romance will never threaten her career again—until she meets superstar anchorman Marc Tyner.

Seize The Dawn
by Vanessa Royall

For as long as she could remember, Elizabeth Rolfson knew that her destiny lay in America. She arrived in Chicago in 1885, the stunning heiress to a vast empire. As men of daring pressed westward, vying for the land, Elizabeth was swept into the savage struggle. Driven to learn the secret of her past, to find the one man who could still the restlessness of her heart, she would stand alone against the mighty to claim her proud birthright and grasp a dream of undying love.

A DELL BOOK   17788-X $3.50

At your local bookstore or use this handy coupon for ordering:

Dell DELL BOOKS   SEIZE THE DAWN   17788-X $3.50
P.O. BOX 1000, PINE BROOK, N.J. 07058-1000

Please send me the above title. I am enclosing $ _____ (please add 75c per copy to cover postage and handling). Send check or money order—no cash or C.O.D.'s. Please allow up to 8 weeks for shipment.

Mr./Mrs./Miss _____

Address _____

City _____ State/Zip _____